Spirit Quest

by Susan Sharpe

Bradbury Press • New York

Maxwell Macmillan Canada • Toronto
Maxwell Macmillan International • New York • Oxford • Singapore • Sydney

*To Henry, Suzanne, and Tia,
who showed us the landscape,
and to
Kate and Alison,
who hiked it with us*

Library of Congress Cataloging-in-Publication Data   Sharpe, Susan.   Spirit quest / by Susan Sharpe. — 1st ed.   p.   cm. Summary: Vacationing on an Indian reservation off the coast of Washington, eleven-year-old Aaron becomes friends with Robert, a young Quileute Indian who is preparing for his spirit quest.   ISBN 0-02-782355-5   1. Quileute Indians—Juvenile fiction. [1. Quileute Indians—Fiction.   2. Indians of North America—Washington (State)—Fiction. 3. Friendship—Fiction.   4. Washington (State)—Fiction.]   I. Title.   PZ7.S5323Sp   1991   [Fic]—dc20   91-4417

Note to the Reader

The Quileute nation are real people whose families have lived at La Push for thousands of years. I have tried to describe their glorious landscape and their ancient heritage as accurately as I can, but I have surely made some blunders. I have been helped by the work of many scholars and writers, especially Ronald L. Olson, George Woodcock, Jay Powell, and Vickie Jensen. My greatest thanks go to Ruth Kirk, who very generously looked at my manuscript and tried to correct my errors. I also wish to thank the individuals in La Push who talked with me about living there today. Robert and his family, like the other characters in my story, are of course completely fictitious.

The pictures in this book were drawn by my daughters, Katherine Sharpe (age 11) and Alison Sharpe (age 8), using black permanent markers or pens on Bristol board. In some instances they followed designs made by ancient Northwest Coast artists; in some cases they imitated contemporary Indian artists, who continue vigorously to use and modify their traditions; and in a few cases they have drawn from their own imaginations, following a Northwest style.

Each chapter opening illustration is intended to reflect the content of each particular chapter. The following spirits and objects are depicted: Thunderbird (Chapter 1); Sun Mask (Chapter 2); Starfish (Chapter 3); Raven Mask (Chapter 4); Sun Mask (Chapter 5); Fish Spirit (Chapter 6); Wild Woman (Chapter 7); Whale (Chapter 8); Eagle (Chapter 9); Eagle with Fish (Chapter 10).

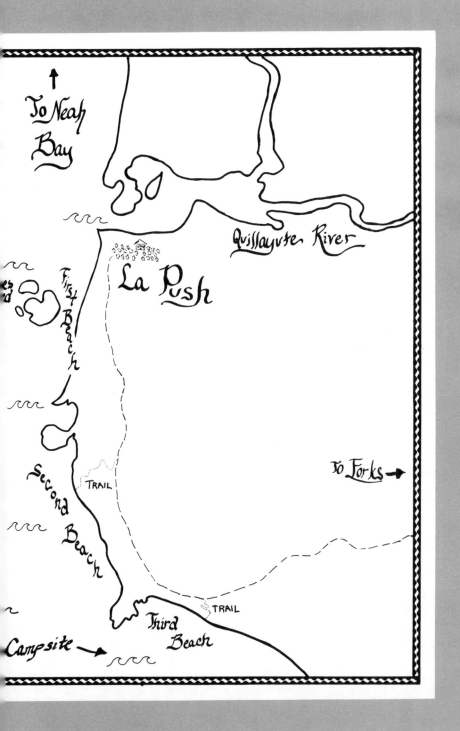

CHAPTER
1

Aaron was reading aloud to his parents from the backseat of the minivan. He was a fine reader, for someone who had just finished the fifth grade; all his teachers said so, and so did his parents, who had shared reading aloud with him since before he could remember.

But something was wrong. He felt cramped, perhaps because his legs were getting too long for the backseat. He had come to the word *pelagic* and it was making him mad. "The Quileute were noted for their skill in pelagic sealing," he read. He hoped his parents couldn't explain it either. "What does *pelagic* mean?" he asked politely.

"Pelagic things swim in open water," said Mrs. Singer, turning her twinkly blue eyes toward him. Sometimes she could be jolly and funny, but sometimes she talked just like a teacher, which is what she was. A college teacher. "As opposed to benthic things, for instance, which live on the ocean floor."

"Okay, *okay*." Aaron brushed his mother's answer away. Why did she always have to tell a person more than he wanted to know? "Anyway," he summed up impatiently, "it says they were great whale and seal hunters. Do you want to hear any more?"

"You're reading very nicely," said his mother. "Isn't he, Larry?"

"Yes, I'm enjoying it, too," said Mr. Singer, who was driving. "But I hope you're not missing the landscape."

Aaron looked out the window again. All he could see were dismal acres of stumps, evidence of the lumber companies at work. Where the forest still stood the view wasn't much better, because the line of dark spruce trees formed a tunnel for the road. "How far is it now?" he asked.

Mr. Singer looked at his watch. "Maybe another hour. Read us a little more, why don't you. That book's not great, but it's all I could find that had anything about the Quileute."

So Aaron found his place again in *Indian America: A Traveler's Companion*. "Salmon constituted an important food, and roots and berries of various kinds were also relied on for sustenance." Riding and reading made him a little sickish and the road had too many curves. "I can't say these words," he complained. "You read it."

His parents laughed. "Poor Aaron is growing up and getting grouchy," teased his mother.

"I am not," he growled. And under his breath he added, "Mind your own business."

"That sounds like a good healthy diet," his father interjected, keeping the peace by changing the subject. "I wonder what they eat nowadays."

"Peanut butter and jelly?" suggested Mrs. Singer.

"Probably they still eat salmon."

"How do you know?" Aaron demanded. "You've never even seen a Quileute Indian, have you?"

"I guess we don't know any personally, do we, Rosalind?" asked Mr. Singer. "It's a very small Indian nation."

"But are they friendly?" Aaron tried to sound

casual, but it was important whether or not he was going to find any friends on this trip. His mother was a marine scientist who often spent the summer, when she wasn't teaching, at one seacoast or another. His father would then take a holiday from the gallery to concentrate on his own painting. Aaron had enjoyed these trips when he was little, but suddenly it was not only his legs that were too big for the car. Although his parents were good people, they seemed to know nearly everything, and maybe they spent too much time with him. Now Aaron felt as if he needed some room to grow on his own. He wanted to hang out with the guys back home, who didn't explain things to him all the time. He wanted to experience something by himself, without his parents discussing what it meant. But here he was, cooped up with them, being dragged off to the coast of Washington, to a small, lonely Indian reservation where the water was too cold for swimming.

"Are the Quileute friendly?" Aaron asked again, since no one had answered before.

"They only take scalps when they're angry," his mother joked.

"Very funny, Mom."

"What does it say in your guidebook?" his father asked.

4

Great. Aaron looked at the book again, but it didn't seem to be describing real people. "Their customs as well as their mythology indicate a possible connection with the tribes of Vancouver Island," he read aloud. "Sure tells a lot about making friends with them. Glad you got me this book, Dad. Thanks a lot."

"Maybe you can do another mythology report for school," suggested his father. Mr. Singer loved to make things educational and Aaron knew he was probably half serious. "You did such a great job with the Greeks. Here's a whole other mythology to learn about."

"It's June twenty-second, Dad. School's only been out a week. I'm supposed to get a vacation, remember?"

"You'll get your vacation. Of course, we can't foresee exactly what La Push is going to be like, but we'll have some good times. I'm sure that some people are friendly and some are not—just like Seattle. Look, this must be the turnoff. Ready, everyone?"

Aaron watched out the front now, curious in spite of himself, while his father slowed down, taking the curves carefully. Across the clear-cuts, wildflowers made bright streaks of purple and yellow and white.

"Do you think Indians still believe their mythology?" Aaron asked. Anxious now that they were so close, he wondered whether, if he did meet an Indian kid, he would really be very strange and different. What did it mean, anyway, to have a mythology? When Aaron had done his Greek report, he had been puzzled over whether anybody had ever actually believed all that crazy stuff about gods on Olympus, getting jealous and starting wars all the time.

"I wonder what the Quileute do believe." Mrs. Singer picked up on Aaron's question. "Of course, a hundred and fifty years ago, missionaries came here, and I think most of the Indians converted to Christianity."

"Sometimes people themselves hardly know what they believe," said Mr. Singer.

"Like you, huh, Dad?"

"Right," Mr. Singer answered with a smile. "I'm sure the Quileute are just like me. Great artists and religious nonconformists."

"And modest like you, right, Dad?"

"Oh look, here we are."

Aaron's father turned the van suddenly onto a driveway and stopped in front of a log cabin with a sign that said OFFICE.

"Mind if I come with you, Dad?"

6

"Sure, come ahead."

Aaron slid open the heavy side door and gratefully stretched his legs to the ground. Beside the office was a large wooden sign with no words on it, just a picture of a creature painted in black and red, with a bird foot, a beak with a long tongue inside, and feathers. But the parts seemed to be all mixed up.

"Oh my, look at that," said Mr. Singer. "That's a picture of Thunderbird. Isn't it handsome?"

Aaron wasn't sure. A good artist, he thought, would make a picture you could understand. But he wasn't brave enough to argue with his father, an artist, about it. He opened the door to the office instead, and found himself before a counter facing an Indian woman. She had long, thick black hair and wore blue jeans and a plaid shirt. She asked Mr. Singer if he had a reservation. Aaron fought an urge to say, "No, you have a reservation" by looking very hard at the postcards that were for sale. He wondered whether there were any kids around eleven years old living in the village, but he was too shy to ask.

All of a sudden, as the woman handed over the key, she smiled at him.

"There's a storyteller tonight," she said.

"There is?"

"Down in the baseball field. You can go. In the tent."

"That sounds great," said Mr. Singer. "What time?"

"Likely around eight-thirty," she said. And she added again, "In the tent."

The Singers' cabin was located near the end of the gravel road, one of a dozen similar places that the tribe rented to summer tourists. It had a ground floor with two bedrooms, and then you went upstairs and found the kitchen and living room, which was all one space, and another bedroom. Off the living space Aaron discovered a balcony. There he caught a whiff of the ocean, and when he listened he could hear the sound of waves, coming through a wall of gray fog. The beach must be visible from the cabin, he thought, when there was no fog. A seagull whizzed out of the gray wall, squawked at Aaron, and whizzed back again. He laughed. Maybe this would be a good place, after all.

"What bedroom do you want, Aaron?"

"Upstairs."

"Why don't you take downstairs, and then we won't bother you if we stay up," said his mother.

"Mom, it's summer, remember? I get to stay up late."

"It's bigger downstairs."

Why did they ask, if they were going to have it their own way anyway? Well, he was getting out of there.

Aaron ran back and forth from the van, unloading stuff, especially his own stuff. He put the tent and the sleeping bags in his room, and he put his father's boxes of paints in the other downstairs room, as his parents suggested. Then he brought a box of food upstairs to the kitchen.

"I'm going to the beach now, okay?" he asked his mother.

"Sure. Be back in half an hour and I'll just make us some hot dogs for supper."

Aaron thumped down the stairs, out the door, and around the cabin toward the roar of the ocean. The cabins made a single row along the line of the beach. But how did you get to the beach? He seemed to be standing in a sandy field full of shrubs, with no visible path. Well, it couldn't be far; he would just head for the sound of the water.

Soon he came to a fallen log, stripped of its bark. Some storm from the ocean, some high tide, had deposited it in this field, he guessed. It was white and smooth, polished by water. Behind it was another log, and then another and another. Aaron followed one of them lengthwise, to try to find a

9

passage to the ocean, but he couldn't see more than ten feet ahead of him because of the fog. Still, he could hear the water retreating down the beach, a moment of silence, and *boom* as the next wave hit. Then, quite suddenly, the logs ended, and Aaron saw smooth sand and water. Just as suddenly the fog seemed to move and a window opened, deeper and deeper. He saw several gulls flying, and then, as the fog parted more, he saw an island, a crazy tall island with cliffs all around and spruce trees on top like hair. A large fishing boat—it must be a fishing boat, Aaron thought, for it had nets hung from steel arms—was chugging silently past the island. Its motor was inaudible in the roar of the waves, so that it seemed like a ghost boat. The beach itself was empty.

There is a wild, open feeling that comes from an empty beach. Aaron felt as if the wind might blow him up into the sky, just as right now the breeze was blowing the fog away, the last wisps retreating around the back of the island. He felt as if he were the first explorer ever to hear the sound of these waves. The irritation he had felt on the trip seemed to be blown right out of him. Here he was, all alone, all on his own! Who knows, he might even discover something here, something his parents knew nothing about, some artifact or Indian relic washed up by the sea.

Right over there, a little ways away, was a shiny spot on the sand. Aaron made for it on the run, frightening a gull into the air. It was a piece of tinfoil.

Aaron put the tinfoil in his pocket, smiling at himself. No point leaving trash on the beach. Maybe some gull would think it was something to eat, and choke itself.

Looking up, he saw, out of the corner of his eye, a movement in the sky. Was it another gull? No, it was a bird, all right, but this one was perhaps the biggest he had ever seen, outside of a zoo. It had a white head and a dark body, with a white tail. From the deep forest behind the cabins, it headed for the water. As it passed overhead, Aaron saw the beak, cruel and strong, the top hooked down over the bottom. He wished he knew what that bird was. It might even be worth asking his mother and father.

Mr. Singer said they could probably walk to the tent to find the storyteller. They went out the gravel driveway, shaded by huge Douglas fir trees, past the office and the Thunderbird, and down the road. There were houses on one side, and a mobile-home park on the other. While some of the houses were nice, some of them made Aaron uneasy. One had a collection of whirligigs in the yard, but another had broken windows. Aaron couldn't tell whether someone lived there like that, or whether the house was just empty. A few of the houses had big satellite dishes for television reception, and one had a dog tied up.

Walking on, they passed a tiny post office and a grocery store with gas pumps out front. From that part of the road, straight ahead, up on a hill where it looked out upon the water, they could see a bright blue house with a sign that said QUILEUTE TRIBAL SCHOOL. Two Indian girls came riding their bikes past the Singers, going fast, the bigger girl carrying her baby sister on behind. Aaron wondered whether they went to that school, and what it would be like.

Finally they saw the tent, set up in a field down below the road. Walking down steps made out of truck tires, Aaron felt shy, although no one paid any attention to him or his parents, except for an occasional polite smile. At the bottom of the steps they passed a long, narrow shape, draped with old gray cloths, which Aaron peeked under curiously. To his surprise, the shape was a huge canoe, big enough for twenty people. It was being carved out of a single log, by hand; Aaron could see where some kind of a tool had made little hollows all over the inside.

When he noticed an Indian boy watching him closely, Aaron dropped the covering and jerked away. He hadn't known the Indians still had special

13

Indian things. Maybe they didn't want strangers coming around, spying on their treasures. Looking for his parents, Aaron was glad when he saw they were sitting near the back of the tent. He slipped in beside them.

Although the tent was filling up—people were talking and laughing—Aaron felt uncomfortable. He noticed that no one spoke to his family. When he spotted a white couple sitting not far away, Aaron was relieved. Then he saw the Indian boy again, sitting two rows ahead. The boy turned around once, glancing at Aaron. He had long black hair held in place by a headband. Aaron looked around carefully. Most of the guys had short hair and baseball caps.

The murmur of voices inside the tent stopped when a tall man stood up at the front. He was dressed splendidly, in a long cape that came to his ankles in the back and that was decorated with big, pearly white buttons that seemed to form the outline of a picture, although Aaron couldn't tell what it was.

The storyteller explained that he was from Vancouver Island, up in Canada, and said that he brought greetings to the Quileute nation. He talked a lot about something he called a "cultural revival" until finally he got around to telling a story that he said he had learned from the old people on Vancouver Island. "This is one of the stories about Raven," he said, and then paused.

Aaron thought that a raven was a kind of bird. He wasn't sure whether he had ever seen one. But when the storyteller said *Raven,* Aaron felt a wave pass over the people sitting there. It was so quiet that you might have thought just one person was sitting there, as if all those people together were magically transformed into one by their listening.

"At that time the earth was dark," the storyteller began, "because one family had all the light, which they kept in three boxes." He said this quite calmly, as if it could be true. Part of Aaron wanted to laugh, but another part of him seemed to be going out to meet this idea. He imagined the earth dark, as it was outside the tent now, and a family somewhere, an Indian family, who had that light in beautiful, decorated, wooden boxes.

"Raven was greedy and lazy, and he wanted all the light for himself," the storyteller went on. "So he planned himself a way to get into that family's lodge. Now this family had a daughter who was as beautiful as the sky, and they would not let anyone marry her. But one day she went to the spring to get a drink of water, and there Raven lay in wait. He turned himself into a hemlock needle and dropped into her cup, and she drank him right down.

"So the girl became pregnant, as Raven grew inside of her, and in due time the baby was born. And this baby, who was truly Raven, would cry at night, and he cried and he cried, after the way of babies, until the family tried everything they could to satisfy the baby. Finally they gave him the first of the boxes, and so he stopped crying, and when they were all asleep Raven opened the box and out flew the millions of stars, out of the smoke hole and up into the sky!" Here the storyteller raised his arms while his cape spread out with the buttons shining like a million stars. The people rustled in their seats, as if they were turning to watch the stars travel up into the dark sky.

"Raven was pleased. And so, on the next night, he cried again, and he cried until they gave him the second box, and once again they fell asleep. Raven opened the box, and the beautiful round moon flew up through the smoke hole into the sky." Again the storyteller's arms seemed to fly up like the moon. "And so on the next night, when he cried for the third time, they gave him the third box, and this time he changed into his true shape right before their astonished eyes, and he took the box in his beak and flew off with it. Now he truly had all the light.

16

"But remember, Raven is greedy and lazy. Still he was not satisfied, and he said to himself, 'I will have all the water, also.' So he went to his cousin Petrel, who kept the water, and he stole that and carried it away, too." Here the storyteller could hardly talk because he had puffed up his cheeks, bigger and bigger, and as Aaron started to laugh he realized that everyone was laughing with him. Then the storyteller let out his cheeks with a great explosion, saying that even Raven couldn't hold that much, "so some of the water spilled—a lake here, a river there. And it spilled on the houses of the First People, who were quietly going about their business, so they ran out and shook their fists at Raven. 'Stop throwing water on our lodges!' they cried, and they called him terrible names.

"But Raven would not stop, and besides he told them that if they didn't stop calling him names he would do something that would frighten them very much. Of course, they didn't stop calling him names, so Raven opened the box that held the sun—" Here the storyteller threw out his arms so suddenly that Aaron jumped in his seat. "And the sun rose up into the sky!" Slowly, the storyteller lifted his arms and looked upward. "The First People were so frightened by the light that they ran for cover. They ran to the bushes and trees, they crawled into holes in the ground, they wriggled into hollow logs and caves, they dived under the water, and some even flew up into the air, completely distracted. . . ."

Here the storyteller paused. It was like being in church. Aaron felt the silence in his bones. It was part of the darkness outside and the faraway sound of the waves on the beach, still coming over and over again.

"Remember that the birds of the air, the fish of the sea, the animals of the woods, all the living creatures that surround us, contain the spirits of the First People. They live still in the places to which the sun has frightened them, and although many are smaller now and have changed their shape, each living thing that surrounds us holds a spirit, if we could only be aware of it."

Aaron thought of the great bird he had seen on the beach. He wanted to shut his eyes and be silent, trying to remember exactly how it looked. But the storyteller was finishing, a light came on from somewhere, and there was clapping and chair folding and clattering as if the whole audience had suddenly fallen into separate pieces. Aaron saw his parents still sitting there, but he felt funny, not having remembered them the whole time.

"What a fascinating story," said Aaron's mother as she blinked in the light.

18

That was when Aaron noticed the Indian boy staring at them. He just knew his parents were going to start discussing the tale. "Mom, watch out," he said. "People are listening."

"It reminds me of another story, in places," said Mr. Singer, paying no attention to the warning. "Like the story the Christians tell. Right, Aaron?"

Aaron tried to walk away from the sound of his father's voice, but in the crowd, with people moving chairs and talking to one another, he seemed to be trapped.

"You know what I mean," Mr. Singer continued. "A story about a baby mysteriously born to a girl. And it turned out to be a god?"

"*I* see what you mean, Larry," said Mrs. Singer. "Isn't that interesting."

Aaron didn't see and didn't care. Outside, he climbed the tire stairs quickly, but at the top he looked back and noticed the boy still watching them. The boy waved, ever so slightly, so Aaron waved back. And then Mr. Singer said, "That was a long drive this morning. I'm tired." He put his arm around his wife's shoulders, letting Aaron get ahead.

Aaron entered the road where the sky was open over his head. They were far from any city, with no moon. The fog must have completely blown off, because each star of the millions was a perfect point of clear light, except where the Milky Way formed a blurry path of brightness. Sometimes seeing the stars made Aaron feel that the earth he was standing on was just another pinpoint, whirling through the cold, empty spaces. But tonight the stars seemed closer and more friendly, as they must have looked whirling out through the smoke hole.

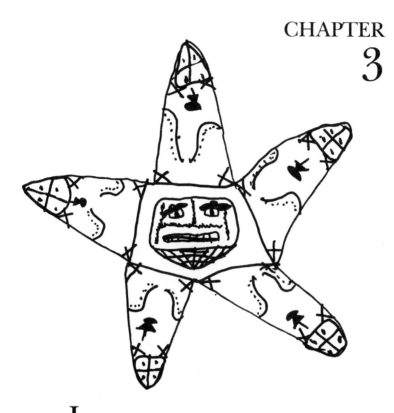

In the morning the fog again took over the view from the balcony. Aaron could see the ground, but he could not see as far as the first of the logs he had climbed over.

"It'll take me half the morning to set up for painting," said his father. "I'll take over that downstairs bedroom, okay, everybody?"

"You're going to make my room smell of turpentine," complained Aaron.

"Well, I'm sorry about that. Keep your window

open. We just don't have the space here that we have at home. Are you going right off, Rosalind?"

"I may as well. Fog won't get in the way. Where's that map? I think I have to drive up to Second Beach, which has the best intertidal habitat. They say it's a bit of a hike in. Do you want to come with me, Aaron?"

Aaron was tempted. It would be fun to go to another beach. "How far is the hike?" he asked.

"Less than a mile, I think."

"You going to count creatures all day?"

"And watch who's eating whom. We could stop for a picnic lunch."

It was tempting, but Aaron decided not to. When his mother went to beaches she became completely absorbed, looking at things that no one else would ever see. This summer she was planning to study the organisms that lived in tide pools. Her work might help people who try to clean up oil spills on beaches, but it wasn't the kind of work that Aaron wanted to hang around and watch for a whole day.

"I guess I'll go into the village," he said. "Do you think anyone would mind if I hang out there?"

"I don't think so," said his mother.

"Maybe you'll find a friend," added his father.

"Maybe," said Aaron. He knew who he was looking for.

22

After breakfast he walked out the gravel driveway under the giant trees. He decided to stop first at the office, in case the woman there volunteered any more information about something going on. But a different woman answered the jangle of the bell on the door.

"Yes?" she asked, without encouragement.

Aaron quickly selected a postcard, feeling in his pocket for a quarter, which she accepted without comment.

Outside, Aaron stared at his card. It said, "Kwakiutl wooden mask depicting Raven," which sounded like last night except the picture didn't make much sense. It showed a wooden carving of a human face, more or less, with four long arms coming out from it. That wasn't the way Aaron had imagined Raven, at all. He put the card in the pocket of his jacket and went on into the town.

A black Chevy with a bashed-up fender drove by. A brown dog looked at him, not barking, not even curious. No one was around. Aaron walked past the school and past a dock, marked by another Indian sign, this one with a fish on it. Beyond was a marina. He stopped uncertainly, his hands in his pockets, wondering whether he was allowed to walk out among the boats.

Then he saw the boy from the night before, riding a bicycle. When he came near Aaron, the boy pulled on his handlebars, making the bike coast on its back wheel. Then he raced on two wheels up the block, made a sharp turn, and did another wheelie back.

"Hi," said Aaron.

The boy stopped. He was a little shorter than Aaron. His T-shirt said "Quileute Days," and he was still wearing the headband.

"What's your name?" asked the Indian.

"Aaron."

"Aaron Singer, right?"

"How did you know?"

The boy shrugged. "My aunt, I guess."

"How does she know?" Aaron began to feel creepy.

"Works in the office."

"Oh." Of course, he should have realized. In such a little place, people would know things. "What's your name?" asked Aaron.

"Robert Greene."

"Oh."

"You got a problem with it?"

Aaron felt angry. What had he said wrong? Maybe his disappointment had shown in his face. Somehow he had hoped that this Indian boy would be more strange. Anybody could be named Robert and do wheelies on a bicycle. "No, of course not," he said. "I just thought, you know, being an Indian and all, I mean, I thought you'd have some other kind of name."

"Like Geronimo?"

Aaron felt stupid, and even angrier. "Well, I didn't know, okay?"

Robert seemed to consider this answer, as if deciding whether it was good enough. It must have been, because then he asked, "What do you like to do?"

Aaron shrugged. "Go to the beach, I guess. Play soccer. Hang out with my friends. My parents made me come here."

"Where do you live?"

"Seattle."

For a short time, Robert was quiet, looking at Aaron in the middle of the empty road. Then he said, "I went to Seattle."

"Only once?"

"So what. You've only been to La Push once."

Aaron tried to smile. "Well, what did you do in Seattle, anyway?"

"We went to the aquarium. And other places." Robert hesitated, drawing a line in the dirt with his toe. "I might go there to live someday. When I'm big. My aunt went there, when she got married."

"The one who works in the office?"

"No, another one."

"Well," Aaron suggested hopefully, "maybe sometime, when you're visiting your Seattle aunt, you could come visit us, too. You could see my father's gallery."

"What would I want to do that for?"

Aaron shrugged, turning away. He couldn't seem to say the right thing. He had taken friends from school to the gallery, and then his father had bought ice cream for everyone. It had been fun.

Robert interrupted his thoughts. "Maybe your parents wouldn't want me to visit," he said.

"Why wouldn't they?"

Robert didn't seem to know why—or want to say why—because he changed the subject. "How come you're staying for a whole month?"

"Because of my mother. She's a marine biologist. She's going to study the things that live in tide pools on Second Beach."

Robert opened his eyes wide. "The tide pools? Oh man, that's weird. There's millions of things there."

Aaron nodded. "She's just interested in them. She won't get tired. That's the way she is."

Robert seemed to be thinking carefully. He gave Aaron a new kind of smile, with a little light shining out of his dark eyes. "Want to go and see Second Beach?"

"Who would give us a ride?" asked Aaron.

Robert smiled broadly now. "Me," he said.

Aaron turned around on his toes with surprise. "You can't drive," he said.

"Want to make a bet?"

"How old are you?"

"Eleven."

"Me, too. But you can't drive until you're sixteen; everybody knows that."

"Who's going to stop me?" asked Robert.

"Don't you get in trouble?"

Robert shrugged. "Maybe. See, I can drive my dad's old pickup. He doesn't know. I drove it almost to Forks once. That's almost ten miles. I wait till he's out fishing in the big boat. My mother never knows, either. My big brother taught me how. Joe is cool, he just got out of the army. He's working on his canoe, because he wants to win at the canoe races, on the Fourth of July. Man, he can win lots of money. He lets me do anything. Don't you have a brother?"

"No," said Aaron, surprised by this burst of information.

"Well, are you coming or aren't you?" Robert let his bicycle fall right where it was, at the side of the road.

Aaron hesitated. He knew that he should not come, but his mind crowded with excuses: It wouldn't do any harm just to go and see the truck. He didn't want to lose this new friend right away. And anyway, who was going to stop him?

He followed Robert farther into the village, to where a rusty old green truck was parked near the water. Its windshield was cracked and springs popped out of the seats. Aaron agreed to climb in. "Not to drive anywhere," he cautioned. "I just want to see what it's like."

The truck felt fine. The high seats gave him a great view. And the key was right there in the ignition.

"Want to hear it start?" Robert asked.

"Sure." Aaron grinned. So what if his parents saw him. Wouldn't they be surprised!

Robert had to sit all the way forward on the seat to reach the gas pedal. He turned the key and pumped the accelerator. The truck roared, lurched forward, and stalled.

"Oh, I forgot." Robert put his foot on the left pedal and shoved at the gearshift. "You have to be in neutral."

"You sure you know what you're doing?" asked Aaron.

"Sure. I just forgot."

"Won't somebody hear us?"

"They'll just think it's somebody else. They

never come to check." Robert turned the key again and this time, roaring and trembling, the truck sat in its place. Revving the engine, he asked, "Wanna try?"

"Well, yeah." Robert crawled over Aaron, who slid into the driver's seat. Since Aaron was a little taller, he could reach the pedals better. As he pressed the gas pedal, the engine fired up nicely. It was easy. "You can really drive all the way to Second Beach?"

"Sure, it's not even a mile. Then we can hike down to see what your mother's doing. If we just stay near the woods she'll never know we're there."

Aaron felt a terrible sinking sensation. He really shouldn't do this. "I think I would get in trouble," he said.

"What's the matter? You scared I can't drive?"

"No," said Aaron doubtfully. He thought how his parents always trusted him to be sensible, just like they were. Well, they didn't know everything. He could simply go for a drive with Robert without their ever finding out. "No," Aaron repeated, "I'm not scared. Let's go."

The boys traded places again. Robert put his foot on the floor and moved the gearshift. "You look out the rear while we back up, okay? Because I can't see."

"Okay," said Aaron again. He couldn't see much himself. "There's nothing there."

The truck lurched again, backward, so suddenly that Aaron was thrown forward. He caught himself on the dashboard with his hands. Biting his lips, Robert stabbed at the floor with the other foot, until Aaron became aware that the truck had stopped. He sat upright again.

"You sure this is okay?" Aaron asked.

"Sure. I got it backed up, didn't I?" Now Robert eased up very carefully with his left foot, and this time the truck started forward more gradually. Eyes wide open, Robert turned the steering wheel hard to the right. The truck was moving onto the road. Aaron swallowed hard. They were off.

Robert started to smile and the lump in Aaron's stomach began to ease. It was true: Robert was driving the truck. They drove right up the street where Robert had been riding his bicycle and started down the road to the cabins. There were a couple of stop signs, but Robert didn't stop. Luckily there weren't any other moving cars.

"You want to try it?" asked Robert.

"Not today," said Aaron, getting more excited. "Maybe tomorrow, though." It looked easy. They were passing the cabins now, and not a soul had seen them. "Show me how the gears work," said Aaron.

"You have to put your foot on the clutch first, down there, see?" Aaron looked down at Robert's foot on the left pedal. And then before he could think about anything, *bang*! The truck was going crazy.

"Hey, look out!" Aaron yelled. "Step on the brake!"

The truck veered off the road straight for a tree. As if in slow motion, Aaron saw that Robert had completely lost control. Desperately he stretched his leg, reaching for the brake pedal, but his foot collided with Robert's, who finally had his in the right place. The truck stopped. It shook and jumped, but it stopped. Stalled. Though the tree was right in front of them, they had not hit it.

"Oh man," groaned Aaron. "What happened?"

"I don't know," said Robert, looking a little pale. "I think we hit a dog. I just went to show you the clutch and then I saw the dog in front of us. She's my aunt's dog. We've got to find her."

"Is that her?" asked Aaron, pointing out to the side. A black dog was looking at them solemnly, slowly wagging its tail.

"Oh yeah, that's her, that's Blackberry. Come on, Blackberry, come on, girl, are you hurt?"

Aaron opened his door and the dog bounded into the truck, licking them both on the face. "I don't think you hit her." Aaron laughed.

"Oh Blackberry, girl, thank goodness." Robert put his face in the dog's hair for a moment.

"But now we have to get the truck out of here," Aaron pointed out. Then he saw a woman looking at them. "Uh-oh."

"What?"

"Someone sees us."

"Yeah, well." Robert looked resigned. "You want to try to drive it back?"

"No," said Aaron. "Hey, you got me into this. I have to go home."

"You said you wanted to."

"But I didn't know you were going to drive off the road and get us in trouble. And here comes somebody." Aaron took a deep breath. A tall Indian man was walking steadily toward them, not smiling at all. It was too late to hop out and go home. Aaron had never done anything this bad in his whole life. He wondered if he could be arrested for riding with a driver with no license. It wasn't the kind of thing his parents would understand at all.

"Oh good," breathed Robert beside him.

"Good, my foot."

"It's my brother."

The Indian man reached the truck and leaned in the window on the driver's side. He was young and handsome, with long hair and a headband like Robert's. "Having a little problem?" he asked.

"I'm sorry, Joe, really I am, I know I promised you I wouldn't, but Aaron wanted to go for a ride."

Joe looked slowly from Robert to Aaron, who was speechless. "I—"

"You staying at the cabins?" Joe asked, not unkindly.

"Yes."

"Well, scoot over." That was all he said. Both boys moved to the right, while Joe climbed into the driver's seat. He started the truck and guided it easily back onto the road, toward its parking place.

"Don't tell Dad, okay," asked Robert softly.

"Half the village saw you, dummy," said Joe. "He'll know before he gets off the dock, without my helping. And you with a new friend, too. A white kid. Shame on you, Robert."

"I'm sorry."

"I'm sorry, too," Aaron managed to whisper. No one had ever called him a white kid before, and he wasn't sure whether he was offended. He was white, of course. He hopped out quickly when Joe stopped the truck. "Bye," he gulped.

Joe caught his shoulder for a minute. "You tell your parents everything?" he asked with a wink.

Aaron looked at him in surprise. Once he

hadn't told them about a D on a math test. "No," he said.

"Robert needs a friend," said Joe. "Aren't many kids here his age. Would be a shame if your parents didn't want you to come here. I'll keep these keys in my own pocket after this."

Aaron smiled. He was probably safe, then. "I'll come tomorrow," he said before he ran off.

Aaron's mother was cheerful and talkative that night as she made dinner. Second Beach, she said, was the most beautiful place she had ever worked, with abundant tide pools. She had already watched a starfish digest a sea urchin, and a raccoon coming down to eat.

Mr. Singer smiled and nodded and listened, the way he always did, and then he turned to Aaron. "And what did you find in the village?"

"It's okay."

"Any children there?" asked Mrs. Singer.

"Yes. There's a kid my age."

"Did you talk to him?"

"Sure."

"What's his name?"

"Robert."

"And what did you do?"

"Not too much. Played. He's only been to Seattle once."

"Is that so?" said Mr. Singer. "My, it must be a limited sort of life, way out here. I wonder where the children go to school."

"I think Seattle is more limited, though," said Aaron.

His father laughed. "Seattle is a big city; La Push is only a tiny village."

"So," Aaron argued. "Kids here might get to do some kinds of things that kids in Seattle would never do."

"I suppose that's right," his father agreed. And then fortunately he began to talk about the beauty of the fog and the difficulty of capturing its exact color with oil paints.

The next morning, as soon as he finished his Rice Krispies, Aaron took off for the village. He did not tell his parents where he was going, only, "I'll be back for lunch." He saw them give each other a look.

"Bring your friend," his father called after him, but Aaron did not answer.

He found Robert riding his bicycle in the same place.

"You get in trouble?" Aaron asked right away.

"Not too bad. Joe said it was partly his fault, for teaching me. I had to help clean out my father's boat."

"Is it fun?"

"No, it stinks." Robert made a face.

"Well, what do you want to do?"

"I don't know."

"Let's go to the beach. Not Second Beach. What's this one called?" Aaron asked, waving past the logs in front of them.

"First Beach." Robert moved his bicycle out of the road and let it drop.

"That's a dumb name."

They ran together past the dock, scrambled over logs, and entered First Beach at the village end. The fog was hanging low today, in fine drops of water that almost felt like rain. A strange hooting sound blew out over the water, every half minute or so.

"Isn't that a foghorn?" Aaron asked.

"Sure."

"But ships don't come in here. What's it for?"

"For the fishing boats. Coming into the harbor."

"What's that island called?" Aaron pointed to the tall one with the trees on top.

"James Island."

"What's up there?"

"You ask too much." Robert looked sideways at Aaron. "But once in school they told us that they used to leave the dead people up there."

"Bury them?"

"No, just leave them. So their spirits could travel."

"Cool. Maybe we could go up there and find bones, or old Quileute stuff."

"No, we couldn't."

"Why not? We could get there at low tide, I bet."

Robert looked mad. "Because if anything is up there, it should stay there."

"Oh." Aaron felt bad again, but he followed Robert along the beach, where the waves were crashing, gulls were flying, and a beach fire built by some hikers glowed orange through the fog.

"Race you down to the stump," challenged Robert. He didn't seem mad anymore.

"All right. On your mark, get set, go." The sand was soft under their feet, so that running was hard and slow. Reaching the stump, they climbed high into the ancient roots and looked far out to sea.

*   *   *

The boys came to First Beach every morning for a week. Sometimes the sun was shining, but often the fog hung in the air, occasionally obscuring James Island completely. They played baseball with sticks and rocks, and they watched the fishing boats come out of the harbor formed by the Quillayute River, and down into the ocean. They cut the bulbs off the giant kelp, and blew into the stem, making a sound like a sick trumpet.

Robert would not come to Aaron's cabin for lunch, but he did ask a lot of questions about Seattle. How big was Aaron's school? What math did they do in fifth grade? What kind of house did the Singers live in? Was his mother a real scientist?

Although Aaron tried to answer everything, he found Robert shy about describing his own life Until the day when they raced a certain stretch of sand three times, and Aaron won each time. "That's because my legs are longer," he explained.

"I don't mind," said Robert. "That's the way Transformer made me."

"Who's Transformer?"

"Remember the story? About Raven?"

"Sure."

"Transformer is what we sometimes call him. He stole the sun and the moon. My grandmother, she's Makah, you know? From Neah Bay. She tells a story a little bit like the one we heard, but different. She says she can't remember it right. But my other grandmother says that Transformer made the Quileute from wolves. That's why we were brave people, whale hunters."

They were sitting together on a beach log, resting.

"Does everybody really believe that?" asked Aaron.

"Of course not. What do you think?" Robert was silent a minute. Then he added, "I do have another name."

"What do you mean, another name?"

"We went to a ceremony, last summer. To give Indian names to the children. My uncle took me, and Joe came, too. My uncle really likes all that old Indian stuff. He says I have to go to the tribal school, not the public school in Forks. Anyway, we went up to Vancouver Island. The Island is cool; they have totem poles up there and everything. And there was this guy who organized it all. He was a Kwakiutl, who studies all about the old ways."

"So what's your Indian name?"

Robert made a strange sound, with deep noises in his throat and a clicking at the end.

"Oh," said Aaron. "You say that really good. Is that what they call you?"

"Nah. My name is Robert, you know, like, for regular. I just *have* the other name. They did all this research about our ancestors, and that's who I really am." He said the name again.

"What does it mean?" Aaron asked.

"I don't know," Robert admitted.

Aaron thought about having a name that would tell who you really are, not your everyday name that everyone calls you but something deeper, that you could be called at some important time. And yet how strange, not to know what it meant. "Too bad they didn't name you Deer-slayer or something like that."

"Shows what you know. The men in our family were whale hunters, not deer hunters. You don't know anything about us."

"Yes, I do," Aaron answered crossly. "I read about the Quileute in a guidebook on the way up here." He stood up and threw a stick into the water. "You ate salmon and berries." Thrusting his hand into the pocket of his jacket, he felt something. It was the postcard he had bought on his first morning.

"Here," he said, shoving the card at Robert. "Anyway, tell me what this is."

Robert looked at the picture and then turned the card over to read the words on the back. "Raven," he said. "Remember, like in the story?"

"But why does he have four arms coming out of his head?"

Robert laughed. "That's not arms," he said. "See, it's a Spirit Mask. Don't you even know what a Spirit Mask is?"

"No. How should I know?"

"Well, that's all right. You should go to one of the museums, like they have at Neah Bay. See, it's a mask for a dancer. They had dancing when we went to Vancouver. Man, it's the coolest thing; you would love it. Joe and me are learning a family dance. My grandfather is teaching us, and my father doesn't even know how to do it."

"Is it hard? Can you show it to me?"

"No, it's a secret dance. I can never show you. It belongs to my family, and if you learned it you would get our spirit power. My grandfather has a special song, too, that he can still sing. You don't know anything about it."

Aaron nodded. He didn't know. "Can you tell me about the Spirit Mask, or is that secret, too?"

"Nah, it's not secret. Anyway that's a Kwakiutl thing. See, the mask, it's hard to tell from this picture, but those arms, like, close up together, to make a beak. So when the dancer puts that on, it's this huge bird's head. And then he has these strings inside, and at the right time he can pull the strings and the beak opens up like that."

Aaron took the postcard back and studied the picture again. Now he could see how it was. "And the face inside is like the spirit that's inside everything?"

"That's right, that's right. Man, you catch on fast. What I want, what I really want, is to go on a Spirit Quest."

"I thought you wanted to go to Seattle."

Robert looked confused for a moment. "Well, I do. But I also want to go on a Spirit Quest."

"How would you do that?"

"Oh man, you don't know anything," said Robert. "You're worse than my aunt. A Spirit Quest is, like, you have to go into the wilderness. In search of your own personal guardian spirit." He paused and looked at Aaron. "I read about it. My teacher at the tribal school gave me this book. It's something the Indians used to do. When you were a teenager, there would be this big ceremony, and you would purify yourself, and go into the wilderness. You had to suffer, and be alone. You couldn't eat, and you would be cold, and maybe get lost. And then you would have a vision of your special spirit. Your spirit would speak to you. And then you would earn the right to wear that mask at the winter dances."

"You mean, like, if you met Raven, and he spoke to you, then that was your special spirit, and you would wear this mask at the dances?"

"Yes. And that spirit would help you for the rest of your life. Like if you were a carver, the spirit would guide your hand. Or if you were a whale hunter, your spirit would give you strength when you threw the harpoon."

"And if you went to Seattle, would the spirit help you there? Like if you needed a job or something?"

Robert looked surprised. "I don't know. I think the spirit would just help you with, you know, spirit things."

"But maybe if you grew up and went to the city and you were sad and lonely, the spirit would help you."

"Maybe," said Robert carefully.

Aaron's heart beat fast, thinking of Robert getting to do all this. "Could I do it?" he asked suddenly. "Could someone who isn't an Indian go on a Spirit Quest?"

Robert looked at him. "I don't know," he repeated. And then he added, "Anyway, they won't let me do it."

"They *won't*? Not even your uncle who took you to Vancouver Island?"

"Nah. They say I'm too young, and anyway they don't remember anyone who ever did that here. But I'm going to do it someday," said Robert.

"They can't stop me. Even if there isn't any cere-mony, and I just do it myself."

"Do you really think you'll find a spirit?"

Robert did not answer for several minutes. Both of them watched while a gull skimmed low over the water, snatched at something, missed, and flew into the air. And then Aaron felt that same movement in the corner of his eye, and looked up. It was the enormous bird again. "Look!" He caught Robert's arm. "Look! What is it, Robert?"

"Eagle," said Robert. He stood up, shading his eyes to watch. "Sure, that's a bald eagle. He lives back there, in the woods. He comes out here to fish." The bird made a slow pass over the water, then rose and circled back, over the trees and beyond, until they couldn't see him anymore. They waited, but he did not come back.

"Well," said Aaron at last, "I'm hungry. Would you like to come to my cabin for lunch this time? My dad keeps saying I should bring you."

"Sure?"

"Sure, why not?"

"I don't know. My mother says not to bother the people in the cabins."

"Well, my dad paints all day. But he stops for lunch, and he talks to me then. He's okay. He's kind of interesting sometimes."

CHAPTER
5

They ate lunch at Aaron's, sitting on the balcony, for three days in a row. Although the Singers had been in La Push for only a week and a half, already Aaron felt that he shared a secret world with Robert. He had not told his parents about Robert's other name, or Robert's trip to Vancouver Island, or how Robert wanted to have a Spirit Quest. He thought he might tell them someday, but for now, he wanted to think about Robert without hearing their opinions or explanations or advice. Sometimes

Robert was shy, and sometimes it was hard to talk to him, but when he did share his world, he made Aaron feel bold and independent. Aaron wished he could get a guardian spirit, as Robert would, a spirit to help him grow up and know his own mind.

Today at lunch Robert was not being shy. He was slouched comfortably on the deck, asking Aaron questions about Seattle again. "You said your father had a gallery. Is it like a museum shop?"

"It's sort of like that. Only it's just paintings, not books and postcards and jewelry and all that kind of stuff. My dad and a partner run it. They sell their own paintings and other people's, too. Sometimes they sell paintings by Indians."

"My mother sold something once," said Robert. "She made a basket, with beautiful whale designs on it. It took weeks. And then she sold it to a woman for a hundred dollars."

"Oh, that's nothing. In the gallery, they sell paintings for about a thousand dollars. Maybe more."

Robert glanced darkly at Aaron. "So."

Aaron knew that he had hurt Robert's feelings. "It's a pretty boring gallery," he said. "Indian stuff is much better. Like the Spirit Masks. Even if you can't tell what they are."

"I can tell," said Robert.

"Can not." Aaron threw a piece of his orange at Robert. "You had to read my postcard to find out what it was, remember?"

"Who cares about that?" answered Robert, throwing the orange section back at Aaron. It missed him and popped over the edge of the balcony.

Aaron giggled. "Bet you can't hit me." He lobbed another piece, but Robert dodged it.

"Hey, what's going on up there?" Mr. Singer yelled.

The boys looked at one another, but neither said a word.

"It's raining oranges down here. Don't you boys have something better to do?"

"Okay, Dad," said Aaron.

"How about—" Robert started, like someone who has a good idea. But he stopped.

"Yeah?"

"I was just thinking. Up at Neah Bay they have this dig, where an old Indian village was, in the old time."

"Oh yeah, my dad told me about that. He said he was going to take me, but he never does. Was it an old Quileute village?"

"No, it was Makah. They have another reservation up there, you know, where my grandmother's from. It's only a few miles up the coast. So what I was thinking was, if there's an old Makah place, then there should be an old Quileute place. If we found it then scientists would come and study the things, and then the Quileute could have a great museum, like the Makah do. It makes them proud; my uncle said so."

"Sure!" Aaron began to see the point. "And if we discovered an ancient village, we would be famous."

"But we wouldn't touch anything ourselves, or take anything," cautioned Robert. "Because those things belong to the tribe. Anyway, the old village should have been close to La Push. But not exactly here, because someone would have found signs of it by now. So what we have to think about is, where else would they have put their village?"

"Well," said Aaron reasonably, "we know they lived on the shore, right? Because they hunted on the ocean."

"Right."

"So the most likely place is—the next-closest beach. Which is Second Beach, right?"

"That's what I think," said Robert. "Let's get Joe to drive us in the truck. I'll get a shovel; my dad keeps a shovel at the house. And we'll dig, not right on the beach but in the woods up above."

"And then we can get a ride home with my mom." It was a wonderful plan, to Aaron's mind, and partly because he would so much enjoy his mother's surprise when she saw them.

They found Joe down near the marina, working on a canoe that was long and thin, with an outboard motor. Joe quickly agreed to drive them up the road in the green truck. When they put the shovel in the back, he said he would not ask what it was for. "You'll like Second Beach," he told Aaron.

"Isn't it just like First Beach?"

"In a way, but more special. You'll see."

Joe left them off in a little grassy parking lot that held the Singers' van and just one other car. A trail led into the woods from the parking lot.

The trees above Second Beach were very large, with curtains of mossy stuff hanging down from the branches. On the ground were large ferns, and padded places, thick with moss and needles, and fallen logs softly rotting with new trees growing right up out of them.

"Sometimes," said Robert quietly, "I think that I will start my Spirit Quest right here, in the woods above Second Beach."

"I think you would be right," said Aaron. A bird called sharply. Aaron thought of Raven, and of the beautiful girl who went to the spring and drank down a hemlock needle. "I think you would find a spirit here." Just as he said that, Aaron's face brushed something invisible and soft, something that clung to his cheek, making him step back with a small cry.

Robert laughed. "You ran into a spider's web," he said.

As Aaron retreated he could see the whole web, a large spoked pattern that ran between a spruce branch and a salmonberry bush. A fat black and yellow spider in the middle had reared up, on the alert. "Is it dangerous?" Aaron asked.

"Nah. Just a spider."

"Look. I knocked part of the web apart."

"He can fix it. Come on, let's go off the path. Like in a Spirit Quest, when you had to get lost."

There were so many huge fallen trees that it was difficult to leave the trail, but Robert discovered a ghost of a path through the sword fern, and they started on that.

"But what if we *do* get lost?" asked Aaron.

"We would have a better chance of finding the remains of a Quileute town. If it was on the regular trail, somebody would've found it by now. Here, you take the shovel for a while."

"All right." Aaron felt a little as he had when he climbed into the old green truck. Was Robert going to make him regret this? They passed huge, shaggy-barked cedar trunks, sometimes so big that you couldn't be sure if you had walked halfway around them and were continuing on in the same direction. The shovel over Aaron's shoulder kept knocking into things or getting caught on the hanging moss or on bushes. No one could walk in a straight line through these woods.

Then, quite suddenly, looking down, he saw a piece of pottery.

"Robert! Come look!"

The boy turned and came back. Together they knelt down and fingered the old, blackened piece very carefully.

"Did the Quileute make pottery?" Aaron asked.

"I never heard of that," Robert answered. "They made baskets and cooking boxes out of cedar bark."

"Maybe they made pottery, too, in the old time, but no one knows about it. I think we should dig here."

Robert agreed. They cleared away the needles and sticks with their hands, in a circle. Aaron put the shovel to the ground.

It was nearly impossible to dig. The shovel hit roots in every inch. But they took turns pounding and cutting with the blade, and gradually dug down, an inch and then another inch. Suddenly, Robert sank the blade halfway in, striking a hard object. "There's something here," he said excitedly.

"Probably just a rock," cautioned Aaron.

"But we need to be careful," said Robert. "If it's an artifact, we don't want to ruin it."

"Let's dig around with our hands," suggested Aaron.

"Good idea." They both got down on their knees now, feeling with their fingers in the dirt, carefully removing handfuls, peeling away the mat of roots.

"Here," said Aaron. His fingers had touched an edge of something. He had completely forgotten about not disturbing anything, and apparently Robert had, too, because he scraped away at the dirt around it, while Aaron kept a tight grip.

"Oh!" Aaron fell backward as the thing popped out. Then he sat up straight to see what was in his hand.

It was a piece of an old tin can, so rusted it had no bottom, but still with rings around it.

"Someone was camping here," said Robert sullenly. "They're not allowed. We should report them."

"Sure we should. From ten years ago. Great idea, Robert."

"Well, you're the one who thought it was a

special sign of an ancient village. I told you Quileute didn't make pottery."

"Well, you were digging, too. And anyway I don't even believe there's any old Quileute village. I'm going to find my mom."

"I bet there is so." Robert stood up anyway and shouldered the shovel.

"Which way?" asked Aaron.

Robert just looked at him. They didn't have to say a word. It was clear they had done it, gotten lost, almost as if that had been their plan.

"The ocean has to be to the west," declared Aaron. He felt proud of himself for that. And he remembered something from school. "Moss grows on the north side of trees. So we find a tree with moss. . . ."

Robert curled his lip, gesturing at the nearest tree. Moss grew on its branches, moss trailed from its top, moss grew like a stocking several feet up the trunk, all around.

"I guess that's in a different kind of woods," Aaron admitted.

"But the sun," suggested Robert. "That's it, we can tell by the sun."

The boys looked at the sky together. Up, up through those tall trees, bending their necks back until they hurt, until they could see the patch of bright light at the top. But the sun was hidden somewhere behind clouds.

"We just have to walk," said Robert. "We keep walking in the same direction, and after a while, we come to something. The trail, or the ocean, or the road."

That seemed right. "You lead," Aaron offered.

Robert shrugged his shoulders, lifted the shovel again, and started out. They walked silently now, watching for something, any kind of a sign, until Aaron thought of something else.

"If it gets too late," he warned, "my mother will be gone from the beach. We won't be able to get a ride home."

"Then we'll have to walk."

"But what about dinner?" And what about how far they might have to walk? Robert didn't answer, and Aaron knew that was because there was no answer.

They proceeded quietly, while a few birds sang from dark places in the woods. Once Aaron was sure he heard footsteps, but he saw nothing. Although they tried to follow a straight path, it was hard. Aaron was glad that Robert had some experience in woods like this. Then, among the bright bird chirps, they heard a lonely, irregular moaning sound: "Oo-oo-o-ooooooh."

Aaron stopped, and so did Robert. "What is it?" Aaron asked, telling himself that he was not afraid.

"An owl. Sounds like a spirit, doesn't it? Some Indians used to think that if an owl called you, you were going to die."

Somehow this idea made Aaron shiver. It was as if the owl were watching them and knew that they were lost. Perhaps it was calling to them with the voice of a spirit. Would it lead them the right way or around in circles? Aaron looked at Robert, who was listening very carefully, his head cocked to one side.

"Oo-oo-o-uh-oooooh."

"Come on, Robert. Keep going, okay?"

"Hush!" said Robert. "Hear that?" He handed Aaron the shovel.

"It's just an owl. You said so."

"Not that. The other sound. It's the ocean. You can hear it! That's it! Come on." Robert was off at a run, before Aaron had time to hear for himself. He dashed after, letting the shovel bump behind him. And then he, too, heard it, louder with every step. *Bou-oom.* The rhythm of waves.

The ground took a sudden dip so steep that Aaron could not stop running and had to catch onto branches to slow himself down. And then, like a small miracle, they were standing on Second Beach.

The wide smooth sand curved around like a half-moon. On each side rose huge sea stacks, islands of rock, with colonies of birds flying and nesting. One sea stack had a hole in it, as big as a doorway, that made you want to run up there and look through to the other side. And the whole beach was wide and empty and beautiful. Too empty. Aaron's mother was not there.

Aaron dropped the shovel. The sun was quite low; what time would it be? Five? Six? Sometimes Mrs. Singer had come back to the cabin as early as four. She seemed to like to sit and relax with Aaron and his dad before they made dinner.

Sometimes she had stayed out a little later, when the tide was right. Aaron wondered whether she ever went on to another beach. Maybe she crossed over one of the headlands, to another place farther away.

"I don't see her," said Robert briefly. He sat down on the sand, puffing after his run.

"Oh *great*. Just fine." Aaron plunked down beside Robert. The sand felt hard and unfriendly. His stomach was starting to rumble. "At least Joe knows we're here. He'll come back for us."

After a pause, Robert said thoughtfully, "He

was going to Port Angeles after he dropped us off. He won't be back until midnight."

"Oh *swell.*" It got cold at night and they didn't have their jackets. Aaron stared out at the sea, so beautiful, so large, so unhelpful.

"Didn't you tell your dad where we were going?" asked Robert.

"No, remember? He was mad about the oranges."

"Oh *swell.*"

Something moved on a sea stack out there. Aaron squinted. The light was wrong for seeing. He forgot himself a moment. "What's that, Robert?"

"Where? On the rock? A seal. See, there's a bunch of them. They often sit there."

"Like the ones the Quileute used to hunt?"

"Sure. And sometimes you see whales here, too. The old-time people would stand up on those headlands and watch for whales."

Carefully now, Aaron scanned the water, and then the rocks. At the north end of the beach there was a great jumble of rocks and tide pools, and then again he saw something move. Something . . . blue!

"It's her!" Aaron leaped to his feet, pointing. It *was* her. Now she stood up, with her blue bandanna and her pack of equipment. She had been kneeling down over there, behind a rock, peering into a tide pool, of course. Aaron's voice must have carried, because she waved her arm at them, starting across the rocks and sand toward them. Aaron could hardly make himself stop jumping and waving to her.

"She sees us, it's okay," said Robert. But he was smiling a broad smile.

Mrs. Singer was delighted to see them, too. She asked them casually how they got there, as if Aaron were in the habit of showing up on his own just any old place. It was four o'clock, she said, time to start home, but she had something special to show them first.

"What?" asked Aaron. He nudged Robert and dropped back. "She's going to explain something now."

"I don't mind," said Robert. "I like it when my mother explains something to me." They followed Mrs. Singer to a nearby tide pool, bumping their heads peering into it together. At first Aaron saw nothing but the usual starfish. But then he saw that something was attached to the bottom, something you could hardly see because it was almost clear, like a plastic tube.

"I suppose it's some new kind of seaweed," guessed Aaron.

"No, it isn't," said Robert. "Look, it's breathing."

Aaron looked, and Robert was right. There

were dark places inside the plastic tube, which moved. And at the top, where the tube branched, a tiny jet of water went out one side, and in the other. "All right, Mom, I admit it, that's pretty weird. So what is it?"

"It's called a tunicate," she said.

"But what *is* it?" asked Robert.

She smiled at him. "It's your grandfather."

"Mom. Be serious."

"When Raven made us," said Mrs. Singer grandly, "he carved us from tunicates. That's why we have backbones." Then she added more seriously, "Odd as it may seem, this creature is an ancient type of almost-vertebrate. His kind have been around a lot longer than we have. And our evolution stems from this thing."

"Ha! You think Indians tell funny stories," Aaron jeered.

"No, I don't," Mrs. Singer answered. "I loved the storyteller."

"I think the tunicate is cool," said Robert. "Can we pick it?"

"No," Mrs. Singer cautioned, "let's leave it be. I don't like to collect anything unless I have a real need for it. We disturb the ecosystems enough as it is."

Robert nudged Aaron this time. "Your mother sounds like an Indian," he said.

"Why?"

"Indians don't take things either, unless they need them."

"But that's because of the spirits. My mother doesn't believe in the spirits."

Robert shrugged. "I don't know. She does the same thing in the end anyway."

Mrs. Singer was packing her gear. "Let's head up the trail," she said. "Who wants a ride home?"

"Me," they answered together.

"And could you carry the shovel?" asked Aaron.

She laughed. "Not a chance. Whatever made you bring that heavy old thing to the beach?"

Fortunately she didn't wait for an answer, and the two boys followed her up the trail. It had steps going up the steep part. Aaron started to count, bounding past his mother. "Fifty-three, fifty-four, fifty-five, fifty-six . . ."

"Sixty, sixty-one, sixty-two," continued Robert, passing Aaron.

"Did the Quileute think," Aaron asked, puffing, "did they think even a tunicate would have a spirit?"

Robert considered. "Maybe," he said. "Maybe it does. Especially if it's really an ancestor. Is that true, what your mother said?"

"Sure it's true. My mother knows what she's

talking about. Only—well, she doesn't exactly mean your grandfather, you know."

"I know," said Robert. "It's like the old stories. It means something but maybe not exactly what it says."

"That's just it," Aaron agreed. "One hundred twenty-six, one hundred twenty-seven . . ." He couldn't talk anymore.

CHAPTER
6

On the morning after the trip to Second Beach, Aaron awoke with an annoying whining, buzzing sound in his ears, which was coming from somewhere over in the village.

His mother had already gone off to catch an early low tide, but his father had heard the noise, too. "Sounds like a chain saw," Mr. Singer guessed, drinking his coffee. "You better go investigate."

That was exactly his plan. As he trotted past the school and the marina, Aaron wondered whether they might be cutting a big cedar to make another canoe. The sound grew louder all the time, too loud for a chain saw, really.

Then Aaron saw Robert standing on the bank of the small harbor. The whining noise flew on up the river, and then Aaron knew what it was: the outboard on Joe's canoe, of course. He joined Robert to watch.

"Tomorrow's the Fourth," Robert reminded him. "Joe's going to Quinault for the races, and I'm going with him."

Aaron thought about asking whether he could come along. The canoe, long and narrow, with a beautiful lift to the bow, came whizzing past them, with an earsplitting noise and a stench of gasoline.

"You can't come," Robert added, before Aaron could ask. "Joe's bringing a whole carload of his friends. And we're going to eat with my cousin there."

"I don't care," said Aaron, though he did. "We're going to have our own fireworks on the beach at night." And anyway, he comforted himself, it wasn't much fun, watching the canoe go back and forth.

The afternoon of the Fourth dragged without Robert. Aaron got tired of sitting on the beach alone and came in to watch his father, who shook his head at his canvas. Wiping his brushes on a rag, he said, "It's not right."

"Why don't you put in some birds?" Aaron suggested. He sprawled in a corner chair, eating another orange and putting the seeds carefully into a box full of dried-up paint tubes. He would never say his father's painting was boring, but it was. It had the colors of a foggy morning, bands of wavery green and gray and blue. But nothing happened in the picture.

"Eh? Birds? Little black dots of things. I can't think how that would help the design."

"Fish, then," said Aaron. "You could make a whale, right there in that blue strip. And a Thunderbird up top, with its wings out. Whale and Thunderbird. That would be good, Dad. Thunderbird used to catch whales."

Mr. Singer turned around, squinting at his son. "What have you been doing?" he asked.

"Playing."

"With Robert?"

"Yeah, with Robert."

"What do you do?"

"I don't know. Go places. Go to the beach. Hang around the dock. Stuff like that."

"I hope you're not bothering anyone."

"We're not." Aaron still thought his father's picture needed a little life in it. Now it was like the world even before Raven, no spirit. When you went to the beach there was always something moving there, the birds wheeling around the sea stacks and sometimes seals slipping off the rocks. And in the tide pools, where the water was so still, you would look and wait and then see that everything was alive, moving very slowly, waving something or creeping along, opening or closing. And in the woods, too, there were spiders and ants and butterflies, and plants growing everywhere, and bugs in the old logs. The world was so alive. Aaron couldn't find words to describe his feeling.

"You could paint more like the Indians do," he suggested, to his father's back.

Mr. Singer turned and smiled. "I thought you didn't like Indian designs."

"Well, I guess I like them more now. After you look at them awhile, they begin to seem better. But I still don't understand why sometimes everything is double."

Aaron's dad nodded, put his brush down, and fished into a pile of paper under some rolls of canvas. "Here," he said. He brought out a calendar decorated with Northwest Indian designs and opened it. Aaron wished he hadn't said a thing, feeling another explanation coming on.

"You see this? We are used to artists who draw

a thing the way they see it. So you get just one side or one perspective, as we say, at a time. But the Indian artists had a different idea. Here, the artist has drawn both sides of this animal at once, do you see? It's as if the creature had been sliced down the middle and spread open like a newspaper."

"I see," said Aaron, although the picture still didn't make sense. "But what are all these lines on the inside?"

"Those represent the internal organs, or maybe bones."

"You mean the insides? They would draw the guts and everything?"

"Right. Because remember, they're not just drawing what you can see."

"Well, it's pretty good. You should try something like that, Dad."

Mr. Singer closed the calendar and set it down, shaking his head. "I've actually thought about it," he said. "I'd like to try a Thunderbird. Of course, I'm not a Native American myself, so in a sense I have no right to those traditions."

"Oh." Aaron did not like the sound of that. "So what if you're not a Native American," he said. "Can't you paint whatever you want?"

"Well, yes, of course, but you know it has a different meaning when an Indian does it."

"That doesn't make any sense, Dad. A picture's a picture."

Mr. Singer looked curiously at Aaron, as if he had just said something very wise. "You know, of course, Aaron . . ." He stopped.

Aaron smiled. "If I know, what's the big deal?"

"Well, you know that the relationship between Indians and whites has not always been, well, to the benefit of the Indians."

"Did the white people come and massacre these Indians?"

"No, at least not intentionally. They came to buy sea otter skins, in the beginning. But they brought in terrible diseases. An awful lot of the coast Indians died of smallpox. And then, when the United States and Canada became real countries, they passed laws against the Indian religion."

"That was stupid."

"Yes. The idea seemed to be that the Indians shouldn't be Indians, they should be white people. It was terrible. The children were forced to leave their parents to go to boarding school. They had to speak only English, and they were punished if they spoke their own languages."

"Yuck. And did the United States have laws against dancing, do you think?"

"I think so, at least if the dancing had anything to do with religion. Basically, the white people wanted the Indians to forget their beliefs and act like whites. They even outlawed potlatching."

"I never heard of potlatching."

"A potlatch was a ceremony where a family gave things away."

"Like Christmas?"

"Not much. A great chief would invite people for a special occasion, maybe when a child was born, or at a marriage. The people accepting the gifts would have to witness or affirm that this really happened, that it really was the chief's son, or whatever."

"But it's not against the law now, right?"

"No, now we've learned a little more sense. But it's hard to undo the damage of several hundred years. And naturally, now, the Indians protect what is theirs. Because their experience with us is not very good."

Aaron finished his orange and wiped his hands on his pants, thinking about Robert and about himself. "Robert never asks me to his house," he said suddenly.

"Well." Mr. Singer nodded and went back to painting. "There might be lots of reasons. Never mind about it."

"Do you think his parents mind him being with me?"

"No, I don't think so. You're kids. I didn't mean to make you worry about it. The Indians invited us to the storytelling, didn't they?"

"Yeah. And Robert told me more stories. Do you think that's a bad thing, me trying to join in on Indian stories?"

"No. A story's a story, right?" Mr. Singer turned a moment and winked.

"But it might have a different meaning. . . ."

"If an Indian tells it. It might. But when children tell it, it has their own meaning."

This idea was so satisfying to Aaron that he sat and watched his father painting, silently, for a full five minutes. And then he continued, "Churches let people visit, don't they, Dad?"

"Certainly," said his father. But he looked a little surprised.

"And synagogues, too. Because you took me there once."

"Sure."

"A person might be just visiting a church or a temple, and they could meet God there, just like a regular member."

"Aaron," his father said gently. "Would you like us to take you to church more often, is that it?

Or the temple? You know your Uncle Jack would be only too happy. Your mother and I really didn't mean—"

"No thanks, Dad," Aaron interrupted. "You don't have to do anything. I was just thinking."

The next morning Robert was back at the old meeting place by the rock. Aaron started right in. "Hey, Robert, I've got an idea."

"What?"

"A Spirit Quest. We should go on our own Spirit Quest. To see if there really is such a thing."

"Of *course* there's such a thing. I already told you I'm going someday. But they won't let me."

"No, but listen. They will. We'll go together."

"You have to go alone." Robert looked cross.

"I know that. I know, for the old kind of Spirit Quest. But this will be, like, our *own* Spirit Quest. People make up their own prayers and stuff all the time. And remember, you told me your uncle said that the old ways have new meaning in new times. Maybe you have to change the ways a little, too."

Robert looked a bit more interested. "They still won't let us," he said.

"Listen, here's what we do. We go for an overnight. Remember I told you my dad promised to take me for an overnight? Well, he never took me.

He doesn't really like sleeping on sand, I heard him tell my mom. So I'll just tell him, Look, you don't have to go, I'll go with Robert. We can't get lost, if we go to Second Beach and start hiking. We'll take the tent, and you can take my dad's sleeping bag."

"We could make a fire," added Robert. "Fires are safe on the beach."

"And we could cook hot dogs. My mom will give us food, she doesn't mind."

Robert was thinking carefully now. "We could," he said finally. "I think they would let us. Maybe your mom would have to tell my mom, okay?"

"Sure. Okay."

"And we can't start at Second Beach. You can't cross over the headland at Second Beach. You have to drive down farther and then you take the trail to Third Beach."

Aaron laughed. "And then you hike to Fourth Beach and Fifth Beach?"

"No, after that they have different names."

"Who gave them such dumb names, anyway?"

"White people." Robert hit out playfully at Aaron, who almost fell in the water. But they were both happy, and spent the afternoon making plans—what they would bring, what they would eat, where they would stop for water.

"Don't forget to ask," they reminded each other at parting.

"Maybe we can even go tomorrow," suggested Robert. "If it doesn't rain."

But they could not go tomorrow, nor the day after, nor any day after that. Not just one parent, but every single one of the four, said no to the boys going by themselves.

"But why *not*?" wheedled Aaron.

"Because it's just too lonely," said his mother. "This is the wilderness, after all. I see very few people at Second Beach, and down toward the Hoh River there would be even fewer. Anything can happen. You could fall, you could burn yourselves in a fire. Dad will take you, next week, before we go home, Aaron. And Robert can come along, too. Right, Larry?"

"Of course. Now listen, Aaron, I was twenty years old before I went backpacking on my own, so just take it easy."

Robert said it was pretty much the same with his family. Both boys knew that going with Mr. Singer, although it might be fun, would not resemble a Spirit Quest in the least little bit. And then it rained for two days.

All that weekend Robert and Aaron sat in the Singers' living room playing an old electronic basketball game, because there was no TV at the cabin.

Mrs. Singer stayed home from the beach, drawing diagrams of starfish and mussels at the kitchen table and complaining about the beeping sounds from the game. Downstairs, Mr. Singer struggled with a picture of a Thunderbird. Aaron was so cross he hoped it wouldn't turn out.

On Sunday afternoon Robert sat up suddenly and said, "How about if we go with Joe?"

"Who?" asked Mrs. Singer.

"My brother, Joe. He's twenty years old."

Aaron felt a surge of hope. Why not? Joe would be better than his dad, anyway. At least Joe was an Indian.

"That way Dad wouldn't have to sleep in the sand," Aaron reminded his mother.

"Joe can even drive us down there," added Robert. "You can get rid of us for a couple of days. Or three. We could go for two nights. Joe doesn't mind. I think. Shall I ask him?" He looked at Mrs. Singer hopefully.

While his mother hesitated, Aaron punched a button on the game for another loud, persuasive beep.

"Stop it, Aaron. I'm trying to think. Maybe that arrangement would be all right. If you boys are really so set on this. Let me see. I'll speak to your father, Aaron, and Robert, you go and check with your parents. Remember, Mr. Singer and I will have to speak with them personally. Joe, too."

Robert grinned at Aaron as he dashed out the door. "Talk to him," Aaron urged his mother. "Talk to Dad right now."

Joe said that he would do it, if the boys promised to wash the dishes. It suited him best if they left on Wednesday, only three days away. He met with Aaron's parents, who said he seemed like a very nice young man. Robert's father said they might as well go for two nights as one.

On Tuesday evening Robert's parents came to meet the Singers. Mr. Greene had short hair and wore a baseball cap. He shook hands with Mr. Singer, saying he ran a fishing boat out of La Push. Mrs. Greene smiled a lot, and Aaron thought she was pretty. She told Mrs. Singer she was happy that Robert had a friend this summer, because she worked at the Tribal Center and it was hard for her son to find things to do. Both of the Greene parents looked at Mr. Singer's paintings and were extremely polite. But Aaron was sure they didn't think much of them.

"Do you really make baskets?" Aaron asked Mrs. Greene.

She laughed. "Did Robert tell you that? I

made one good basket after a hundred tries—I don't have the patience anymore. Robert's learning to make baskets, aren't you, Robert?"

He beamed shyly. "Yeah, they teach us in school."

"He's learning Quileute, too," continued Mrs. Greene. "I can't speak it at all. My mother-in-law spoke the language all the time, but I never knew what she was talking about. And now they teach it at the tribal school. Robert tries to help me pronounce the words." She laughed again.

"So your community is working to save the old crafts and so forth, is it?" asked Mrs. Singer.

"My older son has made a cedar canoe," she replied.

"Oh yes, we heard the outboards."

Mr. Greene laughed. "That's the new with the old," he said. "You won't find me out hunting whales in a canoe. But it takes a little spirit power to find the fish these days." He winked at the two boys.

Aaron's stomach lurched. Was Mr. Greene making fun of them? He couldn't wait to get out on the beach, away from grown-ups.

CHAPTER 7

By Wednesday morning the skies had cleared. There wasn't even a morning fog. In the preceding days, each meal had been carefully planned and packed, and the boys had practiced setting up and taking down the tent three times. At the cabin that morning, they loaded the packs and some extra gear into the back of the old green pickup and squeezed into the front seat beside Joe.

"Wanna drive?" Joe asked Robert.

"Shut up," said Robert with a giggle.

Mr. Singer came out and shook hands with everyone, wishing them good luck. Then Aaron's mother insisted on leaning in the window to give him a kiss. Robert giggled again.

"Shut up," said Aaron, punching him.

"Quit it, everybody, because here we go," said Joe as the old truck shivered its way onto the road. They did not have a long drive before they came to another small parking lot, like the one for Second Beach.

"Want to have lunch before we start hiking?" Joe asked.

"Nah," said Robert. "Let's go as far as we can before we eat."

"It will make your packs lighter," Joe pointed out.

"My pack's not heavy," answered Robert.

"Mine neither," said Aaron.

But the gentle trail to Third Beach was long— through another forest of cedar and hemlock, where fog hung in the high branches. In the darkest places Aaron could easily imagine that the trees themselves were ancient spirits, patient and wise.

When Joe suggested lunch again, Aaron was glad. He sat on a mossy log near a bright yellow fungus.

"Pack gets heavier as you walk," Joe declared.

"Any scientist can tell you that. Picks up air as you go along. You have to stop and let the air out."

"You're goofy," said Robert.

After their sandwiches, they met a party of campers headed toward the road. When Joe asked them how far it was to the beach, Aaron was relieved to hear them answer cheerfully, "Not far at all, you're almost there." Sure enough, soon he heard the waves, and the trail began to drop steeply.

As soon as they reached Third Beach, the boys dropped their packs, took off their shoes, and ran down to put their feet in the water. The cold made Aaron's toes ache. Robert picked up a fat brown kelp stem, waving the rope of it around in the air.

"Can we camp right here?" Aaron called to Joe, who had seated himself on the sand.

"Don't you want to go down to the next beach?" Joe asked.

"Well, maybe *one* more."

"You'll make it," Joe promised with a smile. "The next beach is smaller, more private. And it has a good freshwater stream."

So they hiked again, down the beach to where the next headland cut off the view. Here a trail wound suddenly upward over a steep gravelly slope by means of rope ladders tied to small shrubs and rocks. They had to hold onto a rope while their feet climbed up wobbly wooden rungs. They scaled two of these ladders, entered the woods, and ascended two more. Aaron's heart was racing, from the steep climb and perhaps also from the exposed heights.

Passing under an enormous rock dripping with damp moss, he tried not to look down. How many more ladders could there be?

"Look, Aaron! Hurry up!" Robert was just ahead of him.

Aaron stepped forward and suddenly found himself on a shelf of rock, looking down on the tops of gulls flying over little toy waves.

"Wow! We really came up!"

From here the trail went almost level through the woods for a mile or more, until it wound down again, not quite so steeply, to the little beach that Joe had described. A jumble of crazy sea stacks stood off the shore here, and the beach was all their own.

"Let's sleep right beside the water," suggested Aaron.

"Tide will get your feet wet," Joe reminded him.

"Oh yeah. I forgot." So they chose instead a place that was back near the forest edge of the beach, but not so close that their campfire would be a danger to anything. Joe found some large drift-wood logs and placed them so they would have seats around the fire. Outside the circle, the boys set up their tent. Joe rigged a tarp for himself, saying it wasn't likely to rain that night anyway. The sky was still so clear they could see little specks of birds flying half a mile out over the ocean.

Joe had brought a steak, frozen, in his back-pack. By dinnertime it was thawed and ready to cook. Aaron and Robert gathered wood for a fire. When it was crackling nicely, Joe brought out a long-handled frying pan, put the steak in it, and held the pan over the flames. He told Robert to empty a can of soup into the other pot, while Aaron's job was to find the peas and set the can near the hot coals where they would heat up right.

"And watch they don't tip over," Joe added.

The steak smelled lovely while it cooked. The sun dipped lower and lower toward the edge of the ocean, while some puffins came right close in, floating up and down. A small group of hikers passed by and waved, but no one else seemed to be camping on this beach that night. All the boys could hear was waves and sea gulls, the happy noises of the fire, and then the bubbly sound of the soup. The ocean turned orange and then purple as the sun fell into it.

They had no plates. Robert thought Aaron was bringing them, but Aaron said he was only supposed to bring the forks.

"Never mind," said Joe. "Forks are good enough. Pass one over. Watch it there!"

Too late. Aaron had spilled the peas. As the can hit the fire, the water inside steamed up into the air.

Robert looked over at the peas covered with sand. "I don't like them, anyway," he said.

"Not out of a can," Aaron agreed.

"Here," said Joe. "Have a piece of bread, you two. And don't drop it."

"Joe," said Robert, when they had eaten every little bit and sopped the juice out of the frying pan with their bread. "Joe, did you ever go on a Spirit Quest?"

Joe grinned at him as if Robert were joking. "Who told you about Spirit Quests?" he asked.

"My teacher." Robert's face fell.

"I never did anything like that," Joe explained more seriously. "Remember, when I was your age there was no tribal school, only the public school in Forks. It seemed as if no one was interested in Quileute culture. I don't know all that stuff you know. So tell me about a Spirit Quest."

So Robert explained how you had to go on a

quest for your very own guardian spirit, who would help you for the rest of your life. And how you had to wear no clothes, and go hungry, and eventually the spirit would come to you in a vision.

"You kids thinking of going on one?" asked Joe.

Aaron looked quickly at Robert. He didn't want Robert to tell, because he was afraid Joe would make them feel foolish. And anyway, he felt suddenly as if he didn't need a Spirit Quest. It was beautiful to be here. It had grown dark while they were talking. Sitting in the light space around the fire, Aaron had not noticed until that moment how dark the sky and the water had become. He was glad Joe had told them to set up the tents earlier.

"Not really," said Robert.

"Don't you believe, in the spirits?" Aaron asked Joe.

Joe was quiet for a while, staring into the flames, not saying anything. And then he said, "Listen!"

Aaron heard a rustly noise from the trees far above them, and he heard the forever sound of the waves, *bou-oom,* pause, *bou-oom,* pause.

"Sometimes," said Joe darkly, "you can hear the Daskiya."

"The what?" Robert looked up.

"Grandma used to tell about her," said Joe. "A giant woman, who has kelp for hair and walks in the woods with her huge basket, picking berries and herbs. And if she finds children, she picks them, too, and puts them in her basket. Then she takes them home and eats them."

"Sure," Robert jeered. "Sure she does. They just made that one up. You can tell. They just made it up, to scare children so they wouldn't run away."

"Like the bogie man," said Aaron.

"Well, that just proves you two guys know more than I do," said Joe. "Now, how about the dishes you promised to wash?"

"We don't have any," said Robert happily. "Remember? No plates."

"You heat up water in the frying pan, rinse it out, and then wash the forks in there. Here, just use a drop of this soap. Then you throw the slops way back there, in the woods."

Soon the kitchen chores were done. To dump the dishwater, Aaron had to leave the firelit area and walk toward the dark woods. There the trees seemed to shiver and sigh. He threw the water and hurried back to the safe firelight. Now there was nothing to do but crawl into their sleeping bags. The two boys left the tent flap open while they watched the fire die down. Aaron meant to wait until the glow was completely gone, but the next thing he knew it was light everywhere, and Joe had already started a new fire for breakfast.

"Morning there, sleepyhead," Joe called cheerfully.

Aaron looked over and saw that Robert was already up, too. He drew his legs out of his bag and shivered. It was colder this morning. Pulling his jeans on, Aaron crawled out of the tent. Joe was turning pancakes.

"I'm glad you came," Aaron confided. "Because you make better food than we would."

Joe laughed. "You could cook camp food," he said. "It's not like a kitchen, where somebody has rules about how you do everything. You just scratch your head and figure it out. Here, hold this pan while I stoke up the fire."

So Aaron happily held the frying pan over the flame, ducking his head when the smoke blew his way. Robert came down the beach carrying a canteen of fresh water from the nearby stream and kneeled beside Aaron. "Tonight," he whispered. "We're going to get rid of Joe. So we can be on our own."

Aaron was startled. "How are we going to get rid of him?" Remembering the night, and the comfort of the fire, Aaron wasn't so sure he wanted to be on his own.

"I don't know," Robert admitted. Aaron felt better; maybe they would all stick together.

After breakfast they packed everything up again and continued on. They crossed over another small bluff, and then began a long beach walk around a point.

"How far does it go on like this?" Aaron asked.

"About thirty miles, I guess," answered Joe. "Down to Hoh, where there's another Indian nation."

"Have you ever been there?"

"Sure, we have relatives there. 'Course, we usually drive."

"How far have we come? Are we halfway?"

Joe laughed. "We're probably not six miles yet. It doesn't matter, we're not going all the way anyway. Anytime you find a place you like, we can stop and make camp. Because remember, tomorrow we have to hike all the way out."

So they took it easy. It was hot after lunch, and Joe lay down for a nap in the sun, his head on his pack.

"Let's go swimming," suggested Robert.

"Too cold," Aaron replied. "And anyway, we don't have any suits."

"Who needs suits," said Robert impatiently.

"Skin is waterproof. It's not too cold for me." He tore off his T-shirt, then his shoes, his jeans, and then before he got to his underwear, Aaron was joining him.

"Ouch!" yelled Aaron, as he ran into the cold waves after Robert.

"Come on," cheered Robert, who was up to his waist. "This is part of the training for a Spirit Quest. You had to swim every day. You would get so tough you could swim in the ocean for hours."

"Oh I bet." Aaron cringed as a wave slapped at his thighs. He hoped Robert would chicken out before he had to go any farther. But he didn't. Instead Robert gave a ripping yell and suddenly dove headfirst into the icy water. He was up in a second, grinning, his black hair streaming rivulets onto his shoulders.

"Ha! Bet you can't do that!"

"Bet I can." Aaron forced himself not to think and plunged in. The cold seemed to squeeze his chest, but he came up feeling warm and tingling all over.

"All right, Aaron!" Robert plunged again, and Aaron dove after him. This time it was not as bad, so he swam a few strokes. He felt strong and good.

"Race you to shore!" called Robert. That wasn't fair, because he was already closer, but Aaron ran for the beach willingly enough, pumping his knees through the heavy water.

"Last one out is a rotten— Yikes!" Robert hit the waves with a splash, laying himself flat.

"Are you okay?" Aaron tried to hurry toward Robert now.

"Look!"

Aaron looked up. Three young women were hiking down the beach, watching them. And Joe was sitting on a log, laughing.

The prettiest one waved at the boys, and then all three discreetly turned their backs. They seemed to be introducing themselves to Joe.

"Come on, Robert, run for it." Now they really raced to shore, grabbing their underwear and pants and frantically trying to pull them on over wet skin.

By the time the boys were dressed, the girls were seated around Joe on the log, taking snacks out of their backpacks. Robert and Aaron made a face at each other. They could hear the girls announcing their decision to camp right here for the night.

"Now watch," Robert whispered to Aaron. "Now we've got them for the whole trip."

Aaron rolled his eyes. He stared down the beach, in the direction they were supposed to be hiking right now. They were almost at the next headland.

Suddenly Robert pulled Aaron away from the others. "Aaron, come here. Don't say anything yet. But in an hour or so, when it's almost time to make camp, we tell Joe we want to camp on the next beach, over that headland, see? It isn't far at all."

"That's it!" exclaimed Aaron. He forgot about the night, and about spirits. It seemed a grand adventure, to camp alone. And of course Joe really would be right nearby, in case anything bad should happen. Which wasn't very likely.

"And Joe will want to camp here," Robert continued. "So let him. There's only hot dogs for tonight, and we can divide them up."

Joe was hesitant when the boys told him about the plan. "I promised your parents I'd stay with you," he kept repeating.

"You are with us," Robert pointed out. "It's just over there. They didn't say you had to sleep exactly next to us."

Christine, the prettiest girl, smiled at Joe. "Give the kids a treat," she said. "*They* don't want you."

"Plenty of room on the beach for two tents," added Susan.

So that settled it. Within ten minutes Aaron and Robert had divided up the hot dogs and the rest of the bread and were scampering down the beach, before Joe had a chance to change his mind.

CHAPTER
8

When they reached the headland, all they could see, at first, was a pile of rock, like a small mountain. They could not see the trail over the top.

Then Aaron said, "But look back here. At all the footprints. People must come this way."

"That's it," agreed Robert. Now they could just make out the worn places on the rock, the little piles of sand and broken shell left by other hikers' feet. Up they went. This headland was craggy, rough, and steep. They had to hold on with their hands.

"I wonder if an old-time Quileute ever went over this way," mused Aaron.

"I wonder if they would go places like this on a real Spirit Quest."

"They might be afraid they'd fall off or something. I mean, if they were all alone."

"I'm not afraid, anyway."

"Me neither," said Aaron.

When they came to the top, there was enough flat space for both of them to sit. A breeze was blowing and they could see far, far out to sea, over the waves that came rolling in such long lines. This new beach was much smaller than any of the others and completely empty. It had another freshwater stream flowing across it and another pile of driftwood logs up against the forest. Everything they needed for a campsite.

"Let's have a snack up here," suggested Aaron.

Robert agreed. "It's like being a sailor up on a mast," he said. They ate a couple of oranges, and then the candy bars they had been saving for a special time.

"If you were on a real Spirit Quest, what do you think you'd find?" asked Aaron.

"Me? I don't know. But I like owls; sometimes I think my spirit will be an owl."

"But what about my spirit?" Aaron wondered.

And then he added, "I wonder how the spirit would speak to me."

"It might give you a Quileute name," said Robert.

"Yeah. But how would I know what it said? I mean, it wouldn't speak in English, for sure."

Robert looked a little puzzled. "I don't think it would speak Quileute, either. I don't know. I don't think it would use words."

"No," Aaron agreed. "But I think a person would know what it meant, all the same."

Suddenly the sun appeared from behind a low band of clouds, making a bright pathway across the water that was hard to look at. At first Aaron thought he saw a movement out there, but then he decided it was spots in his eyes. Looking down, he gathered his orange peels into a plastic bag.

"You better pick up your trash," he said, pointing at Robert's peels and the candy wrapper that the wind was tugging from under Robert's foot. "You can't leave that stuff around."

"I wouldn't do that." While Robert gathered up his garbage, Aaron glanced out to sea again.

"Look!" he cried. "And look there!" It was a spout of water. And then he saw a dark shape—no, lots of them, dark curves that would rise up in the water, roll forward, and sink down.

"What is it?" Robert shaded his eyes.

"Whales, Robert! It's whales; we're seeing a pod of whales!" Aaron jumped up, calling and pointing. "There! And there!" He felt Robert tugging at his shirt.

"Sit down! Sit down, dummy. You're going to fall off the rock."

Robert was right. Aaron had been dancing at the edge of a cliff, paying no attention. He sat down. The boys watched until the whales wheeled away, far out into the ocean.

"We actually saw whales," Aaron kept saying as they scrambled down the rock on the other side. And he had another secret thought, that he was too shy to tell Robert. Maybe, if he did have a spirit friend, it was a whale. But he was afraid Robert would laugh at the thought. And he couldn't really say that the whales had spoken to him, at all.

When they reached the small beach, Aaron's watch showed that it was after five o'clock, so the boys made camp while there was still plenty of daylight, as Joe had taught them. They were careful to get the tent pegs planted deeply in a place where the sand was firm. It might rain that night—white puffy clouds were rising high over the land.

They laid out their sleeping bags and gathered sticks for a fire, just like the night before.

Together they even managed to drag a couple of logs for benches, although they were not as nice as the ones Joe had found. They each wanted to be the one to light the fire, so they agreed to light their own matches on opposite sides. Aaron lit the smallest twig he could find, but the little flame blew right out. Robert's match did better, because he started with a crumpled-up wrapper. Soon a jolly fire was going, which reminded them of food. Right away, they slid their hot dogs onto sticks to hold over the flames.

"Pretty soon the stars will come out," said Aaron happily.

"Unless it's too cloudy."

"Oh yeah, I forgot." Aaron looked up. The sun was behind clouds now, and the sky was dark gray.

The boys were very hungry and ate everything they had, hot dogs and bread and carrot sticks and cookies, leaving nothing but a couple of granola bars and some powdered juice. After breakfast, they had better be on their way home if they wanted to eat!

"Do you think the tent will leak, if it rains?" asked Robert.

"Nah. It's a good tent."

"Maybe the Daskiya will come and eat us up."

94

Aaron giggled. "What do you think the Daskiya would look like?"

"Real big."

"With red eyes."

"Long fat kelp hair. Dirty."

"She'd smell bad."

"Yeah, especially her teeth. When she opens her mouth to bite you, you faint from the smell of her breath."

"Yeah, and she wheezes from smoking. Her breathing sounds like this." Aaron sat up straight by the dying fire and did an imitation of the Daskiya breathing. He made rattling sounds in his throat and then he added snoring, piggy noises in his nose.

"Yeah, like this." Robert sat up and did it, too. They made a great breathing racket together until they were out of breath. But for some reason, they both stopped at the same moment, silent.

But it was not silent. Outside the brightness of the campfire, where the light of the day had nearly vanished, came a sound, low and raspy. A scuffling noise followed, then silence.

Aaron and Robert looked at each other. They could hear the waves, too, very calm now, just a quiet lapping on the sand. And then between the wave sounds, very slow, the low sound that seemed to come from an unearthly throat.

"What is it?" whispered Robert. His hand seized hold of Aaron's shirt.

"I don't know."

"There's no such thing."

"I know."

And yet they sat there, frozen. Aaron's mind raced. He could hear his heart beating now. Could it be a bad crazy person, trying to scare them? It did not sound like a person. What should they do? Into his mind, all unwanted, came vague pictures of spirits, which he pushed aside angrily. No, he did not believe. He thought of his mother, so reasonable, so curious, picking up a starfish, looking so carefully. He thought of his father, painting colors just exactly as he saw them, a little more gray, a little more green. No, there could not be spirits.

"Come on," Aaron whispered. He tugged Robert with him. "I'm going to find it." He stood and stepped away from the brightness of the fire. Looking toward the water, he saw there was still plenty of evening light. And there was a dark shape, near the water, like some large sand castle with a turret on top.

"Is that what made the noise?" asked Robert, pointing.

"I think so."

Walking cautiously forward, they soon saw

96

that it was not a sand castle. The shape moved, just a little. The boys stopped. Silence. Aaron pushed on again. He must know. And then he saw that the thing was a very large bird, with a white head and white tail. Aaron stepped closer. Why did the bird not fly away? Now he could see the animal's beak, large and fierce, the top part hooked down over the lower, and then Aaron even saw strong yellow feet with sharp talons. The yellow eye was rimmed with black, and it was looking at him keenly.

"It's an eagle," Aaron whispered.

"Yeah. Wonder why it doesn't fly away?"

"Better not get too close."

"It isn't even walking. It's just looking at us."

"Maybe it's hurt."

They came a step closer, to within a couple of feet of the bird, but it only looked at them. Suddenly they were startled by that low throaty sound. "Look," said Aaron. "He's got something around his beak. Like a string or something."

"And on his foot. Look."

"Everywhere! Look, Robert, the poor bird. He's all tangled up in it. What is it?"

"Fishnet!" said Robert with disgust. "I saw that happen to a gull once. He was all tangled up and he couldn't eat, he was almost starved. My dad had to hold him and cut the line to set him free."

"Do you think we could cut this one loose? You have a jackknife."

Robert shook his head. "This isn't a gull, Aaron. It's an eagle. I never even saw one up close before. They're fierce! Hey, he could snap your finger off."

The bird's yellow eye had not blinked. "Will he die if we just leave him?" Aaron asked.

"Sure. He can't get food. Maybe he can't even drink. That's probably why he's here, near the stream. Trying to get fresh water."

"We have to do something. Robert, we have to." Aaron took another step toward the bird, ignoring Robert's warning. With a tremendous struggle, the eagle shuffled away from him a few inches. "Come on, eagle." Aaron put out his hand. "I'll help you. I won't hurt you."

"Watch out!" Before Robert had the words out, blood was already dripping from Aaron's finger. He squeezed down on the pain, amazed. There stood the bird, cold, watching, still, just as before, and yet in a split second, almost faster than eyes could see, he had shot out that neck and ripped a piece of skin with that beak. "All right, all right," said Aaron. "Listen, we have to get help."

"Are you okay?"

"It's all right. It'll stop bleeding in a minute. I mean for the eagle."

"We could go back and get Joe," suggested Robert.

"If one of us could hold him, hold his head. . . ."

"Joe has a big knife with him. And that heavy jacket. We could put the jacket over our hands to protect them. I'll go back and get him."

"It's dark."

"I'll take the flashlight."

"Sure? You can get over the headland?"

"I'm going right now. I'll be back in half an hour, don't worry. It's not far." Robert ran for the tent, and a moment later he was waving good-bye with the flashlight. Aaron sat down on the sand near the bird.

The night was as black as a movie theater. No stars, no moon. The fire had already gone out, and the little beam of the flashlight was swallowed up in space.

CHAPTER
9

The wind began to blow. Soon Aaron was barely able to make out the shape of the bird, hunched at the edge of the sea, its feathers ruffled by the wind. Terrible thing to happen to a bird. Aaron thought that the eagle must know that people could help it, or why would it be staying here with him, like this? Maybe it had even been calling out to them, before, when it made the noises. Now it was silent.

Still, it had bitten him. Did it know who he was, or not?

"We'll take care of you, eagle," Aaron said. "Robert went for help. He'll be back soon." Aaron shivered. His hurt finger throbbed a little. He wished he had brought his jacket from the tent.

The eagle shifted back and forth on its feet, once. Maybe it was thirsty. Maybe it couldn't drink with the line over its beak. But maybe it could, maybe it just couldn't fly or even walk over to the stream, to get water. Aaron stood up carefully and looked toward the tent. He couldn't see it, but he could see the pale silvery driftwood behind, and he knew approximately where it was. He walked carefully toward the spot, feeling with his feet so he wouldn't trip over a rock or a stick. Then he heard the tent flap in the growing wind, and reached out and touched one of the aluminum poles. He felt around for his jacket, which he had left right there in the doorway, and then he felt for a cup. He couldn't find a canteen, but he guessed he could fill the cup at the stream.

Listening for the sound of the water, he noticed the wind was pretty strong now, making noises in the trees behind the beach, lonely wilderness noises that made him wonder what other animals might be living all around him, invisible, hiding from his humanness and the bite of the wind. He walked carefully, toward the stream, until he heard the trickling sound and was able to dip his cup into the running water. The wind almost blew the water out of the cup, but Aaron held it against his side and went back toward the waves.

At first he couldn't find the eagle. Had it gone, somehow?

"Eagle!" he called out loud. The wind seemed to blow his voice away, over the empty beach and the noisy waves. "Hey, bird! Where aaaaaaare you?"

He listened intently, and sure enough, he heard the low throaty noise. It was over to his left. Was that the same place? Then Aaron saw the bird again, its head down, its shoulders hunched. Very slowly, he approached as near as he dared and set the water down. The eagle's head came up. It seemed to inspect him and this strange object. Aaron backed away.

"It's water, eagle. Can you drink it? It's for you, eagle. I got it for you." Suddenly the bird was lit up as if by a flashbulb; Aaron saw clearly the keen eye and the beautiful clean white tail feathers and the cruel hook of the bird's beak, and even the beach beyond and the white crest of a wave curling over, and for a split second Aaron thought the bird itself was glowing with magical light. Then thunder rolled down all around, enclosing the two of them in a cave of thudding noise. It was lightning. It was going to storm.

The thunder rumbled away, and for a moment the wind died and the wave ebbed out and it was silent. "Drink, eagle," said Aaron.

The eagle stepped over to the cup, slowly, unnaturally, its legs half tangled. How would it know that this was water? But it knew. The bird put its beak into the cup. It seemed to struggle, there was almost a shake in the body, and then it arched its head high again. And again, it repeated the same action, and again. It was drinking! It was very thirsty.

"Good for you, bird! You're going to be all right, bird! Robert's going to come with help, eagle." But just as Aaron capered and crowed these words, another loud crack steamed through the air and lit the bird drinking. The wind grabbed a flap of Aaron's jacket and threw it into his face, and then the rain came. It sounded like footsteps running over the beach, and at first Aaron thought Robert was coming. Then he was wet, completely wet, all in an instant. He felt cold water on his neck and he felt the cotton jacket suddenly stick to his shoulders. Crouching down, he held his knees with his arms.

The eagle seemed to do the same thing. It tried to tuck its head under its wing, like a little songbird, but it could not lift its wing at all because of the netting. It was a miserable sight, such a magnificent creature standing in the rain beside a plastic cup, the rain beating hard on its feathers, its head bowed low. And no one to help it but Aaron.

Very slowly, Aaron slid the jacket off his arms and walked toward the bird. He held the jacket in front of him, so that if the eagle pecked at him again he might be able to block it with the cloth. When he was within a foot, Aaron stopped and watched carefully. He waited for the wind to pause a moment, and when it did, he threw the jacket over the bird.

He wasn't sure it was the right thing to do. But an eagle would fly up high into a tree and have protection from branches, he reasoned. It wouldn't stand out in the rain and wind. Maybe an eagle could catch cold.

Whatever it was, right or wrong, the eagle accepted it. It did not try to throw the jacket off. And now it was an even more formless shape, hunched in the darkness. Aaron felt like the last person in the world.

Now he began to get colder. The rain still fell; the thunder seemed to get farther away, the lightning less frequent, but the rain still fell. Now he could hear the stream swollen and loud. Aaron held his knees again and shivered. Perhaps he should go back to the tent.

He hated to leave the eagle. Why didn't

Robert come back? It must have been much more than an hour by now. But maybe Robert was climbing when the rain came. Aaron tried to picture the steep trail over the headland, in the dark, with the wind blowing and the rock wet, maybe slippery. For the first time, he was fearful for his friend.

The rain tapered to a drizzle but the wind got colder. Aaron was soaked through. When his teeth chattered once, he went back to the tent.

As he made his way up the beach once more, he realized how good it felt to move. Then he paused. Where was that dang tent, anyway? Why couldn't he see the dark shape of it against the driftwood?

He looked until his foot hit against something soft and heavy. He felt with his hand. The tent, of course. Blown over. Blown over and sopping wet, and he would never be able to put it up in the dark, alone. A new feeling, like despair, came over Aaron. He was cold, he was tired, he was all alone. He knew that if he got too cold something very bad would happen. He was supposed to be drinking hot drinks and putting dry blankets around himself. Ha! Who could even start a fire now, with everything soaked?

He wanted to cry. He wanted his mother and father to come and get him right away.

But they were not there; they did not know.

Aaron tugged at the tent. He would not cry. He pulled the tent along behind him, all the way back to his place a few feet away from the bird.

"Are you awake, eagle?" he yelled. His voice was angry now. It was all the fault of this stupid eagle. No sound came from the dark shape.

"Well, wake up, big shot, and keep me company! What do you think this is, some kind of Boy Scout picnic or something?" The sound of his own anger cheered him.

"Why don't you help me unfold this tent? You could be some help, you know. Instead of just standing there. You're supposed to be pretty strong, aren't you? Listen, this tent is heavy when it's wet. Now I brought it all the way down here, the least you could do is help me set it up."

Aaron realized that he sounded like his father when he was exasperated. He smiled at himself. And now the tent had become a sort of blanket, and he crawled in under it. Immediately, Aaron felt less wet, only damp, as the tent blanket sheltered him from the wind. His body began to make a warm spot the way it did in his sheets on winter nights.

"It's all right, eagle," he said more quietly. "I'm warmer now, thanks. You can go back to sleep. I'll just wait for Robert; I'm sure he'll get here. I'll

106

wake you when he comes, okay, eagle? And then you can get free, won't you like that?"

He talked along for a while, stopped, talked a little. The eagle made no more sounds, but Aaron knew he was there. And he believed the eagle knew that he was there, too. Maybe they were very different, but a creature is a creature. They were both cold, they were both tired, they both needed something to shelter them. And company. That was the real thing. The company, the knowing that another creature was there, waiting this out with you.

"Don't die in the night, eagle," Aaron whispered.

Even after he fell asleep, it seemed that in his dreams he knew the eagle was there, waiting, hoping everything would be all right.

"Aaron!"

He moved his head a little. There was sand in a corner of his mouth.

"Aaaron! Hey, Aaron!"

The eagle, the eagle was calling.

Aaron opened his eyes.

"Look, he's over there! On the sand! That's him."

It was a faraway voice, a woman's voice, and Aaron was awake in the early sun on the beach. He raised his head. Two people were walking toward him. He sat up. His jacket was still there; had the bird moved all night? It might be dead. Aaron stared at the shape. Was the bird still standing, or had it fallen over?

"Are you all right, Aaron?" Someone was running toward him. Now he remembered. It was Joe, of course, and behind him, one of the girls from the day before.

"Sure." Aaron's voice cracked from sleep. "I'm all right. Did you bring something to cut with? Did Robert tell you about the eagle?"

Joe looked at Aaron, laughing. "You crazy kids," he said. "You send Robert over a cliff in the dark, you half froze last night in the rain, but you want me to save your eagle. All right, where is he?"

Aaron felt a moment of guilt. "Where's Robert?" he asked. "Is he all right?"

"He'll live, but I'll tell you, you crazy kids have no business climbing over headlands in the rain. He could have been killed, do you know that?"

Aaron hung his head. "I guess we didn't think," he said.

"Well, he's all right. He had a fall, though. I think he sprained an ankle. He can walk a little, but I wouldn't let him come back over here. Luckily he fell down on that side of the headland, so I heard him call for help. He wanted us to come right back here for you, but I promised him you'd be all right here, and we might not. You don't climb over headlands in the dark."

"I'm sorry," said Aaron.

"So how about the eagle, anyway? He fly away on his own, or what?"

Aaron pointed toward his jacket. It was so still, it looked as if he had thrown it over a stump of driftwood.

"That's him?"

Aaron swallowed hard. "Yes," he said.

Joe stared. "You mean you threw your jacket over him?"

"I thought it might be cold. It can't fly. To cover, you know."

Joe nodded thoughtfully. "You have a head on your shoulders," he said. He took off his own heavy jacket, drawing a granola bar out of a pocket. He threw the bar to Aaron, who smiled thankfully and tore the wrapper off.

"Now," said Joe, looking thoughtfully at the unmoving shape on the beach. "This is going to be a little dangerous. The thing is probably weak, but they don't lose their spirit. You put your hands in the sleeves of this jacket, like this. Good. Now you're going to pull that jacket back off the bird, fast, and stand right there on the side where he can see you, not too close. Christine, you stand there on the other side. I'm going to have to work fast. Can he move either wing?"

"No. He can move his feet a little, and he can drink. But he's pretty bad."

"All right. That makes it easier, in a way. I never thought I'd mess with an eagle. Ready? All right, go!"

Taking a deep breath, Aaron whipped off the jacket. The eagle was alive. Aaron looked straight into its eye and knew at once that it was alive. But it looked weak, almost defeated, raising its head slowly, blinking at them, making no move to get away.

"Say, Aaron, this guy's far gone."

"But you've got to try to help him, Joe."

Cautiously but firmly, Joe put one arm over the bird, holding it in a tight hug. Then he began to cut with his knife. First he did the legs. Nip, nip, the strong fishing net relaxed immediately. Three cuts around the wings, and suddenly the bird struggled, feeling itself free.

"Help me!" roared Joe. Christine, startled, tried to hold the bird by the legs. Bravely, Aaron grasped it right around the beak. Cut, cut.

"Stand back! One, two, three, now!" All three of them let go at the same moment. For an instant the bird froze, but its body seemed to gather itself, feel itself. The head came up higher than before.

"Stand way back!" Joe pulled at Aaron's shoulder, backing him off. The wings flexed once, and shot outward. Aaron gasped. So big! The bird was so big, so very powerful! It stood there a moment, both wings spread out wider than Joe was tall, trembling like a foot that has gone to sleep and comes back all pins and needles.

The eye sharpened, looked once at Aaron, and then the wings beat the air.

"He'll make it!" roared Joe.

The wings made a windy sound, beat once, twice, three times, and the feet of the bird rose over their heads, then higher and higher. The eagle circled over them, ten feet up, testing the air, feeling its strength. Then up, up higher, and smaller, and higher, it sailed on air out over the ocean, and back, and out to sea, and then up into the trees behind them, and was gone.

Aaron felt tears in his eyes, but wiped them quickly away. "Will he be all right?" he asked.

"I think so," said Joe. "If he got water while he was stuck, he should be all right."

"I gave him water."

"You did? And he drank it? Well, for a crazy white kid, you know, you're all right." Joe grinned and clapped him on the shoulder. "Want another granola bar?"

Aaron took it. But while he ate, he gazed again and again at the last spot over the forest where the eagle had disappeared.

Robert was sitting between two of the girls, who were making him hot chocolate and letting him have all the marshmallows he wanted in it. He didn't seem to be suffering too badly. Aaron's conscience lifted wonderfully at the sight.

Joe, however, was worried about how to get Robert out of there. The boy could walk, but his right ankle hurt him, and Joe wanted to make sure that he used it as little as possible. He redid the packs, which were lighter now anyway, so that there was nothing for Robert to carry. Aaron had to take Robert's sleeping bag. And the three young women agreed to hike along with them, helping as they could.

"I'm glad we didn't come any farther than this," said Joe. When Aaron had lifted his new pack to his shoulders, he agreed.

They all had plenty to tell, though, to make the trail seem shorter. Robert explained how it just started to rain when he was a few steps up the headland, and the rain made the rock slippery with mud. He couldn't hold the flashlight and still get a good handhold on the rocks, but without the flashlight he couldn't see where he was going, and even so he thought he had gotten off the regular route. He tried to hold the flashlight in his mouth, but it was too big. Then the lightning came, and he was afraid of being up so high where he could be hit, although the flashes helped him see his way. He had actually put the flashlight away in his pocket when something happened. He thought he was stepping on black rock but it turned out to be empty darkness. And down he fell.

"Lucky you didn't hit your head or something," said Aaron. "Were you afraid?"

"No. Yes. I don't know. My palms hurt a lot, where I scraped them. My foot didn't hurt that much, until I tried to stand up."

"So what did you do?"

"Just . . . called out." Robert gave Aaron a secret grin. "Like there might be a spirit or something to help me. I didn't know Joe would hear, because I didn't know I was that close. Lucky, huh, Joe?"

"Let's talk about lucky when we get your foot X-rayed and find out it's not broken. And when our parents don't ask what you were doing on the other side of a headland, anyway."

After a time Aaron lagged behind the others. He stopped to take a stone out of his sneaker, half on purpose, just to be alone. When he reached the lookout spot on the last headland, above the ladders, a familiar shadow caught the corner of his eye. And then he saw it, the eagle, flying out over the ocean, circling, waiting, soaring. Another bird was hovering over the water. The other bird dove, splashed, came up, a fish wiggling in its beak. Like a fighter plane, the eagle dove for the smaller bird, snatched the fish sharply, and was away with it, circling back for the woods.

"Hey!" cried Aaron in greeting. Then he felt embarrassed. He looked down toward Third Beach, but the others had already headed toward the last trail and did not appear to have heard him. So he yelled again. "Hey! Are you my eagle? Or are you just any old eagle?"

The bird passed right over him, the fish still

wiggling in its claws, and was gone over the trees. Aaron waited, watching. Would it come back? Would it give him a sign? Nothing happened. The small bird returned, circling the water, looking for another fish. The waves rolled at the shore. "Hey you, eagle!" Aaron roared at the sky. Nothing but solid blue, and the dark line of evergreens.

And then without thinking, he started down the ladders that took him to Third Beach, hurrying to catch up to the others. But it was a long way to the parking lot. He soon found Joe and Robert resting together. Joe had stopped to carve a crutch out of a bent stick, and after that Robert got along better.

On the way home, Robert and Aaron got to ride in the back of the truck, with the packs. It was bumpier back there, but Robert had his sore ankle all wrapped up in a blanket so it wouldn't get hurt more. All three young women squeezed into the cab and smiled at them from the back window. It was too noisy to talk.

When the truck turned in at the tourist cabins, Aaron's parents were standing right there beside the roadway, on the lookout. They waved as the truck came in sight, until it stopped and did its old shiver and shake in front of them. Aaron stood up, but of course Robert did not.

116

"Here come the campers!" said Mrs. Singer cheerfully. "But"—peering into the back of the truck—"what's wrong with Robert? Oh my word, he's got his leg all wrapped up! Robert, what's happened?"

"It's nothing, Mom. I mean, I don't think it's broken. He walked pretty good, most of the way out."

"What do you mean, pretty well? Oh, I was afraid something would happen!"

"He looks happy; it can't be all that much of a disaster," said Mr. Singer. "Tell us the story, Joe."

But Aaron told the story, because he did not want it to seem as if Joe was in any way to blame. "Me and Robert wanted to camp by ourselves," he said. "We had a special . . . we wanted . . . anyway, we did; we told Joe we'd just go over the next headland. He was right nearby. But we found this eagle that was all tangled up and then the storm came. . . ."

"I knew it! Larry, I told you they must be having a thunderstorm on the beach, too."

"Hold on, Rosalind, and let him tell the story."

Aaron finally got it all out, more or less, while Joe apologized handsomely for not keeping closer tabs on the boys. He threw Aaron's pack out of the truck and climbed back in quickly. "Can't keep our own parents waiting," he said. "After I take these women back to their car, we'll go to Forks to get an X-ray for Robert."

"Will you come back tomorrow?" Aaron asked.

"If he's okay, he'll be back on Sunday to say good-bye."

"'Course I'll be back," said Robert. The truck growled again and crawled off toward the village.

"So," said Aaron grandly, turning to his parents. "How have you been?"

His mother laughed. "We missed you."

"But I finally did a painting I like," said his father.

"Do we really have to leave on Sunday?"

"Yes, we really do. I thought you were all hot to get back to those Seattle friends of yours."

Aaron found, in fact, that he was eager to get home. When Saturday morning came he did not mind packing his things, though he didn't see why his mother had to clean everything so much. She even made him sweep under his bed, which was just as well because somehow the book called *Indian America* had fallen under there. He laughed when he pulled it out.

He went to give it to his father, who was

about to pack up his paintings. "Can I see the good one?" he asked.

"Sure you can." Mr. Singer lifted a canvas lightly off the easel and turned it around, and there it was—a picture that showed, not exactly what La Push looked like, but that was just like La Push, all the same. It had the gray of the fog, the dark green of the forest, and the different blues of the water. It was a picture that seemed to go deeper and deeper, as if it were not really painted on flat canvas but was a real place that you might go into. And deep inside, near the center, was a Thunderbird, drawn somewhat in the Indian way, and somewhat in his dad's own style.

"It's nice, Dad."

"Well, I hope I got the spirit of it at last. The picture's too wet to move. I'll have to set it on top of everything in the van."

"The reason it's good is because you finally put in something that's alive."

"Is that it?"

"Did you know that living things are very important in Quileute mythology?"

"Yes, I guess I had heard something like that." Mr. Singer was groping around in his paint box for the tiny little screw tops for the tubes of paint.

"Most people don't believe in mythology anymore."

"No, most people don't. Check that box over there, would you? There must be some more of these dang little tops."

"A lot of things aren't so much anymore. There used to be more Quileute living here."

"Ah, here's one."

"And there used to be more bald eagles."

"Yes. What did you say that was on the beach, the thing that Joe cut free? Was that an eagle?"

"Yup. And Dad, it was completely tangled up. It could hardly move. And I gave it water to drink. I probably saved its life. Did I tell you that?"

"You told me. And it was a fine thing to do. Maybe living things are very important in Aaron's mythology." Mr. Singer screwed one last cap into place and threw the tube of yellow into the box.

Aaron looked at him to see whether he was serious, but it was hard to tell. "Have you asked your mother whether she has any more jobs for you?"

"Hey come on, she said I could go when I was finished with my own room. You want to inspect?"

"That's all right then."

Robert showed up the next morning while the

Singers were packing the car. He had a fancy new bandage on his foot, but he was allowed to walk. His ankle was only sprained, he told them.

"My parents said I could visit you in Seattle sometime." With a stick, Robert drew a line in the dirt beside the van.

"They did? That's cool. You can visit my dad's gallery. He has a great painting of La Push. I hope he doesn't ever sell it. And if it's winter you can visit my school. It's pretty nice."

"And we can go to stores, and everyplace?"

"Sure. Here, I wrote our address and phone number, so you won't forget."

Robert folded the paper and put it in his pocket. Mr. Singer was already in the driver's seat, growing impatient, while Mrs. Singer banged the cabin door shut and climbed in. "You left the keys on the counter. We're supposed to drop them at the office. Aaron, say good-bye and get in."

Aaron rested his hand on the van door handle, as if he were about to open it. He wished Robert didn't look so sad. "Good-bye, Robert. If you see the eagle, yell at him for me, will you? When I'm old enough to drive I'll come here and we can both go to Vancouver Island for the dancing. If they let me come."

"Why wouldn't they?" asked Robert.

"Because, you know. I'm not an Indian."

"It might be all right," said Robert. "Maybe they'll give you an Indian name."

"Like Geronimo?" Aaron teased.

"Hey, get out of here!"

Aaron slid onto the backseat. As the minivan pulled away he turned to look at Robert one last time, standing there waving under the fir trees, with the ocean booming behind him. He realized that Robert belonged to La Push, more than he would ever belong to anyplace. And even if Robert did come to Seattle, he would always know that this place was here for him, with the bones of his ancestors lying on James Island, with the gulls flying up where the river runs down, with the waves singing on the beach, with eagle and seal, salmon and whale. It was Robert's home. Still, Aaron hoped that a little bit of the spirit power would follow him in his own life.